"Two women in as many days seems slightly—excessive."

"No, Ellie," he drawled. "Two women in *one* day is excessive!"

Her head went back defensively. "May I remind you that you also propositioned me two evenings ago?"

"But you didn't take me up on it."

"You still made the suggestion!"

"I didn't realize who you were then."

Ellie stiffened at the insult she could hear in his tone. "And what difference would it have made if you had?"

Daniel looked at her consideringly. "A lot," he finally answered. "You aren't my type of woman, Ellie. I like my women to be soft and feminine and—"

"Clinging! What are your other requirements?"

"Thinking of applying?"

CAROLE MORTIMER says: "I was born in England, the youngest of three children—I have two older brothers. I started writing in 1978, and have now written over ninety books for Harlequin Presents.

"I have four sons—Matthew, Joshua, Timothy and Peter—and a bearded collie dog called Merlyn. I'm in a very happy relationship with Peter senior. We're best friends as well as lovers, which is probably the best recipe for a successful relationship. We live on the Isle of Man."

Books by Carole Mortimer

HARLEQUIN PRESENTS
1727—WAR OF LOVE
1793—THE ONE AND ONLY
1823—TWO'S COMPANY

Carole Mortimer

One-Man Woman

Harlequin Books

TORONTO • NEW YORK • LONDON
AMSTERDAM • PARIS • SYDNEY • HAMBURG
STOCKHOLM • ATHENS • TOKYO • MILAN
MADRID • WARSAW • BUDAPEST • AUCKLAND

For Peter

ISBN 0-373-11863-5

ONE-MAN WOMAN

First North American Publication 1997.

Copyright © 1996 by Carole Mortimer.

This edition published by arrangement with Harlequin Books S.A.

® and TM are trademarks of the publisher. Trademarks indicated with
® are registered in the United States Patent and Trademark Office, the
Canadian Trade Marks Office and in other countries.

Printed in U.S.A.

CHAPTER ONE

WHAT was she *doing*?

It was like something out of one of those farces that used to be on television years ago. Her sister Beth loved that sort of humour, but the only thing about them that appealed to Ellie was the precision timing as the actors and actresses disappeared out of the main room into cupboards and adjoining rooms immediately before another performer made an entrance. *That* Ellie was able to appreciate—but because it was clever, not because it was funny.

And this wasn't funny.

Not when she was the one who had just disappeared inside the wardrobe!

And only just in time too. Because she could hear the sound of footsteps as the occupant of the hotel suite approached the bedroom.

She could have brazened it out, of course. In fact, she wished now, secreted in the wardrobe as she was, that she had done so. But when she had heard the key turning in the lock of the adjoining lounge she had panicked, hadn't been able to think of a plausible reason for the owner of the hotel to be in one of the guest's suites at eight o'clock at night. But by the same token, she thought now, crowded between two rather expensive-looking suits, what excuse could she give for being found in his wardrobe? The woodworm excuse had already been used in a more recent comedy programme that Beth liked to watch, and Ellie didn't think dry rot would sound any more convincing.

If only she hadn't panicked in the way she had when she'd heard that key turning in the lock! What if Daniel Thackery, the guest in this suite, had left something inside the pocket of one of these suits? He had told her earlier, when she'd booked him in, that he would be dining at the hotel this evening, so he had probably changed before going downstairs. In fact, it had been because Ellie knew he was dining at eight o'clock that she'd thought this would be a good time to come in here. Her timing stank. As did her hiding place. Her first choice had been the bathroom, of course, but there was absolutely nowhere to hide in there—and if Daniel Thackery had decided to go in there...!

He was coming into the bedroom now. Ellie could see his feet through the slats of the wardrobe door—expensively shod feet, the black leather shoes looking handmade. Which they probably were, Ellie realised disgustedly. As was the black evening suit she could see as far as waist-high, the angle of the slats making it impossible for her to see any higher.

Not that she particularly wanted to see his face. She had seen that earlier, when she'd booked him into the hotel. Too stunning-looking for his own good—and that of every woman between the ages of sixteen and sixty, Ellie had decided. Piercing blue eyes had looked at her steadily but without any real interest, his nose was aquiline, he had a firmly sensuous mouth above an arrogantly jutting jaw, and slightly overlong dark hair, brushed back in a carelessly fashionable style.

But Ellie doubted that the expression on that face would be as smilingly uninterested as it had been earlier if he were to open the wardrobe door and find her hiding there!

She wouldn't be too happy herself either if—

'Make yourself comfortable,' he called out in a husky voice. 'I just have to make a quick telephone call.'

'Angela?' drawled a throatily female voice.

'Of course,' Daniel Thackery drawled drily.

Oh, God, he wasn't alone, was all that Ellie could think at that moment!

'Oh, dear,' the woman continued lightly. 'She would be very upset if she realised the two of us were here together.'

'Do you really care?' Daniel Thackery derided.

'Not particularly,' the woman confirmed in a bored voice.

He chuckled softly. 'I thought not. I shouldn't be long. Help yourself to a drink from the mini-bar while you're waiting.'

'OK, darling,' the woman accepted lightly. 'But don't be too long; I'm longing for my dinner,' she added with husky persuasion.

Well, at least they were still going to dinner! For a few moments there Ellie had had a terrible feeling that she might have landed herself in a worse position than she had originally thought she had. What if Daniel Thackery had brought that woman back here to—

to—? There was no way Ellie could have stayed hidden in the wardrobe with that going on in the bedroom!

He was fully inside the bedroom now, closing the door behind him to walk over and sit on the side of the bed, his back towards Ellie, his shoulders broad in the black evening jacket, that overlong dark hair brushed over his collar.

If Ellie could have stopped shaking long enough she might have been able to appreciate—in an abstract way, of course—that Daniel Thackery was a very attractive-looking individual. But as it was taking all her energy to stop her teeth from chattering too loudly with fear of discovery all she knew at the moment was that he was in the room—and she wished he weren't!

Especially as she could now see what she had come looking for. His briefcase. Standing neatly beside the bedside table. All she wanted was one brief little glimpse inside there, to see if what she suspected was true.

Beth had an altogether different reason for wanting to know what Daniel Thackery was doing here—an emotional reason—and it had been because of that very emotion that Ellie hadn't thought Beth the right person to come up here. Now that this had happened she was more than a little relieved that Beth hadn't been the one; much as she loved her younger sister, she knew Beth would have given herself away. And then God knew what would have happened! It would—

'Hello, Angela,' Daniel Thackery drawled as his call was answered, turning to lean back against the headboard, swinging his legs up onto the bed.

With his shoes still on, Ellie noted. Really, some people had no respect for other people's property. This might be a hotel, but even so...

'Yes, of course I'm back in England,' he answered drily now. 'I'm well aware the wedding is next week. No, you don't need to send me an invitation.' His expression hardened along with his voice. 'As one of the key participants, I think I'm well aware of the time of the wedding and exactly where it is! Just organise everything with your usual efficiency, Angela, and trust that I will be there, at your side, at the right time.'

The man was getting married next week! Ellie gave an alarmed glance towards the closed bedroom door. 'Darling' was in the other room, waiting for this man to take her out to dinner—and God knew what afterwards—and he was in here on the telephone talking to his fiancée about their wedding next week! And he didn't exactly sound thrilled at the prospect either. Not that Ellie was so surprised by his attitude; it fitted in with what she already thought of him. She detested men like this—men who thought—

'OK, fine.' He sighed heavily now. 'I'm sorry too. I agree, this attitude is nonproductive for everyone involved. Yes, Angela, I love you too. Take care. And I'll see you next week.' He put down the receiver on conclusion of the call, then put his folded arms behind his head, his eyes narrowed, his expression enigmatic, obviously deep in thought—until a sudden sneeze, quickly followed by another one, had him sitting up on the side of the bed again, his expression now one of deep irritation.

Ellie was glad of the diversion—couldn't quite believe the telephone conversation she had just overheard. Daniel Thackery wasn't even going to bother seeing his fiancée until the wedding next week. What sort of—?

Her attention shifted back to him as he slowly stood up, her restricted view still only allowing her to see up as high as his waist. He just stood there, making no effort to leave the room. Why didn't he move? Leave the bedroom. The hotel suite. The hotel!

She breathed a sigh of relief as she saw that he was finally moving—that relief quickly followed by dismay as she saw him bend down to pick up the briefcase before crossing the room. That must be the reason she hadn't seen the briefcase earlier; he must have taken it out with him, and now he was taking it out with him again. Damn! He—

Her breath caught in her throat once again as he came to an abrupt halt in the middle of the room, turning slightly before taking a step towards the wardrobe. Oh, God, no. He *had* left something in his suit earlier when he'd changed. And now he was going to open the wardrobe door, find her here—and all hell was going to break loose!

'Darling?' A knock on the bedroom door accompanied the woman's call. 'We're going to be terribly late if we don't go down now.'

'I'll be right with you,' Daniel Thackery called back.

Ellie could almost feel the warmth of his breath through the slats of the door as he stood so close to her now. Her own breathing seemed to have stopped seconds ago and not resumed. She could see his hand now, a long, slender hand, the nails clipped short, reaching out towards the wardrobe door. Oh, God, he was going to open it!

What was she going to do? What was she going to say to him? Would she need to do or say anything? The chances were he would take one look at her and call the management. And she *was* the management! When he finally called the police the only explanation she would be able to come up with would be that she had wanted to look inside this man's briefcase—through his private and confidential papers. They would lock her up and throw away the key!

This man was Daniel Thackery—an entrepreneur of world renown. She very much doubted that the police—or even Daniel Thackery himself—would believe that the only papers in his briefcase that she had any interest in were ones that might concern her family. If there *were* any such papers. Which she wasn't convinced of at all.

Beth had been the one to go into a panic when a secretary had telephoned the hotel a couple of days ago and booked a suite for Daniel Thackery for an unspecified length of time, claiming that it would all depend on 'how long it takes him to conclude the business he has in the area'. Because Beth was convinced that part of that 'business' was the acquisition of this hotel!

Beth had met Daniel Thackery at her wedding to James just over a year ago—the other man was an old friend of James's from their schooldays. And she remembered a conversation she had had with Daniel Thackery at the reception given downstairs in one of the function rooms about the hotel business, and how impressed he had been with the efficient running of their hotel, and how he'd said it was a business he was interested in getting into himself. And now, knowing that they'd overstretched themselves financially because of an extension to the hotel, and that they were actually in danger of losing the hotel altogether if they didn't very quickly do something about it, Beth was convinced that Daniel Thackery, being the opportunist that he undoubtedly was, had come here to snap up their hotel.

In itself Beth's theory wasn't too convincing as far as Ellie was concerned—their small, seventy-bedroom hotel was surely not in the league Daniel Thackery liked to play in. But aside from Beth's argument that it wasn't a business he knew, only one in which he wanted to get in on the ground floor, was the fact that James and Beth had separated a month ago and James was privy to the seriousness of their financial dilemma—information he could have passed on to his friend Daniel Thackery. Beth also had a second worry, Ellie knew, and that was that Daniel Thackery perhaps had some information concerning James's possible divorce proceedings.

Anyway, in the end Ellie had felt she had no choice but to come up to Daniel Thackery's suite and at least make a token show to Beth of having a look around. Because if she hadn't she knew Beth would have done it herself. And, considering Beth's emotional state since her separation from James, that definitely was not a good idea in Ellie's opinion. To Ellie's mind, there was still hope for Beth and James to sort out their differences, and she certainly didn't want her sister to add fuel to the fire by being caught spying on one of James's friends.

Although it was strange the way Daniel Thackery was carrying the briefcase around with him everywhere... Maybe Beth's idea concerning the hotel wasn't so far-fetched after all. Well, if Daniel Thackery thought that just because they were financially stretched at the moment he could make a move on their hotel he was going to have a fight on his hands; this hotel was Ellie's life.

But talking of hands—that slender hand was on the wardrobe door now. He was going to open it. And he was going to find her crouched here like an—

And then he sneezed again. And again. And again.

Ellie had noticed him sneezing earlier in Reception, when she'd handled his booking. Perhaps he was coming down with a cold. Ellie didn't particularly care what had caused the sneezing fit; all that concerned her was that it had distracted his attention from the wardrobe. She watched through the slatted door as he moved to the dressing table to take a tissue from the box there.

He continued to sneeze as he walked over to open the bedroom door, and a pair of long, silky-covered legs joined his in the doorway.

'Are you starting a cold?' the woman asked concernedly.

'I don't think so,' he dismissed slowly.

'It's a bit late in the year for hay fever,' the woman teased throatily. 'I hope you aren't allergic to me, darling.' A teasing pout could be heard in the voice.

'I'm sure I'm not,' Daniel Thackery answered with certainty. 'Come on, let's go and have some dinner; we've wasted enough of our evening together already.'

The woman's throaty laughter floated along the corridor as the two of them walked to the lift. Ellie stayed in her hiding place, giving them plenty of time to go downstairs before attempting to leave the safety of the wardrobe.

The wardrobe! She disgustedly admonished herself as she finally all but fell out of the confined space, impatiently pushing back the heavy swathe of fiery red hair that grew straight to her shoulders, with a full fringe stopping abruptly above sparkling emerald-green eyes. She was not short by any stretch of the imagination—five feet nine inches tall in her bare feet—and it felt good to be able to straighten up to her full height after the cramped conditions in the wardrobe. But then, one hardly expected to have to spend any length of time inside one.

Unless 'one' had been caught where 'one' wasn't supposed to be!

It all seemed so ridiculous now. She had only come up here at all in an effort to stop Beth making a fool of herself. And had almost made a complete one of herself!

But, whatever Daniel Thackery's reason for being in their hotel, he was hardly likely to leave incriminating evidence lying around in his suite. And to have looked inside his briefcase—even if he had left it behind, which he hadn't—would have been a criminal offence. It was bad enough that she was in the suite at all without any real reason for being there, but there was no way, she freely acknowledged now, that she could have snooped around in his personal belongings...!

Although she might as well turn the bed down now that she was here. She could tell Doris, the maid, not to bother with the suite, that she had done it herself while up there for another reason. She didn't have to say what that reason was!

It was a large double bed, and as Ellie turned back the quilt and top sheet she couldn't help wondering whether she ought to turn the other side down too; she doubted Daniel Thackery would be spending the night alone. Her anger towards him returned as she thought of the way he had gone off for the evening with 'Darling' after talking to his fiancée on the telephone. The man was unprincipled!

Which made her wonder if perhaps Beth wasn't right; if he was completely without morals in his private life, then surely he must be doubly so in his business life...?

She was willing to accept the possibility that maybe he was here for a reason—and she intended finding out what it was!

'You didn't see anything that—well, that might have given the impression James had sent him? About the divorce,' Beth added with a grimace.

The younger of the two sisters, Beth was nothing like Ellie to look at. She took after their mother, with her short stature and fragility of looks, her hair short and blonde. Ellie had always looked more like their father, who was a tall red-haired man.

'I told you,' Ellie replied irritably, the two of them now seated in their private sitting room at the back of the hotel. 'I didn't see anything.' It had been difficult to do so inside the wardrobe! 'Although I very much doubt Daniel Thackery is the sort of man to be "sent" anywhere.' She could visualise his arrogant face all too easily, and knew instinctively that Daniel Thackery did no one else's bidding but his own. 'By anyone!' she added with feeling.

'Besides, it's only a matter of weeks since James left; he can't be thinking of divorce already.' She frowned as Beth didn't look convinced. 'Is that really what you think Daniel Thackery is here for? I thought you said he might be after our hotel—'

'Oh, he is interested in buying into hotels,' Beth dismissed with an uninterested wave of her hand—a hand still adorned with her engagement and wedding ring. 'I just thought that if there was any information in his room concerning this hotel it would also mean he must have spoken to James recently, and—'

'I think I'm beginning to get the picture,' Ellie interrupted wearily.

The two of them were able to take this short time off because this was the quiet part of the evening for them; dinner was being served and the bar was open at the front of the hotel, and most of the guests were in either of those two places or had actually gone out for the evening. Daniel Thackery and his guest were now in the dining room, Ellie had been pleased to note when she'd got downstairs a few minutes ago.

'Beth, James isn't going to divorce you; he loves you,' she said with certainty, convinced that whatever difficulties her sister and her husband were going through they were only temporary; the couple had been in love since the moment they'd met, and had been married—happily, most of the time—for the last year.

'But if you really think Daniel Thackery may have seen James during the last four weeks, why don't you just ask the man? You know him, don't you?' she prompted reasonably, still shaken from her narrow escape in his suite earlier.

'Not exactly.' Her sister shook her head slowly. 'I've only met him once, and that was at the wedding just over a year ago. He's always so busy that James sees him rarely himself, although he did enjoy the couple of years he worked for him. So we haven't met up with him again since the wedding. Why don't *you* ask him?' Beth suggested frowningly, chewing on her bottom lip. 'You've always been so much more forward than me, and—'

'Because I don't know the man at all!' Ellie pointed out impatiently. 'If you remember, I missed the wedding completely because I was rushed into hospital at the last minute for an emergency appendectomy—'

'I offered to cancel the wedding—'

'Don't be silly, Beth; I wasn't complaining, just explaining,' Ellie dismissed irritably. 'The wedding had been planned for weeks; you don't cancel something as important as that just because one of the guests can't make it.'

'That guest was my sister!' Beth protested.

'And I talked to James and persuaded him that going ahead with the wedding was the right thing to do,' Ellie sighed.

'He shouldn't have listened to you.' Her sister shook her head. 'He—'

'Beth, I don't really think it matters who was or wasn't at your wedding, when the two of you now seem to be talking of divorce— Oh, God, I'm sorry.' She was instantly contrite as she saw the way her sister paled; she had always had an uncanny ability to say the wrong thing at the wrong time! It was the reason why she was still unmarried at twenty-seven, according to her equally straight-talking mother; no man was strong enough to brave her vitriolic tongue long enough to fall in love with her.

'But, Beth, the wedding is unimportant now, can't you see?' she continued more gently. 'It's a fact that I didn't meet Daniel Thackery there, and it now appears he has returned to our hotel and we have to be wary of him on two fronts. But I certainly can't just march up to him and ask him outright what he's doing here!' She frowned deeply.

Beth's expression lightened. 'I don't see why not; it's what you would usually do!'

But Ellie acknowledged that Daniel Thackery wasn't the type of man she usually met; she was sure he would just turn round and tell her to mind her own business. And she would have no choice but to do exactly that. She would also have alerted him to the fact that they were curious as to his reason for being here and thereafter he would be on his guard, which wasn't going to help anyone.

'Do you know what I think we should do—*you* should do?' she corrected pointedly. 'Invite the man to dinner with the two of us,' she announced triumphantly. 'It has to be you, Beth, because you know the man and I don't,' she said persuasively as she saw that her sister was about to protest at the idea. 'He was a guest at your wedding, is a friend of James's, and as far as I'm aware you haven't even said hello to him yet.

'I accept you're a bit wary of him,' she added hastily at Beth's increasingly dismayed expression. 'But it would be perfectly natural for you to invite him to dinner in the circumstances, whereas it would look damn funny if I did the inviting—a woman who doesn't know him from Adam!' Besides which, she still felt very uncomfortable about her presence in his suite earlier this evening. He couldn't possibly know about that, of course, but she did, and she was going to find it difficult facing him again.

Beth still didn't look convinced. 'I doubt that he will stay here very long—'

'Then make the invitation for tomorrow evening,' Ellie interrupted impatiently, standing up to smooth down her straight black skirt to its just above the knee length. 'I have to go and take over in Reception for the rest of the evening now, so I'll leave you to think about it. But if you really want to know if he's at least seen James I think dinner would be the best way of finding out.'

This last remark was perhaps a little below the belt on her part, but if they were to find out Daniel Thackery's motive for being in the area someone had to make a move, and as she'd pointed out, it would look odd if *she* approached him with a dinner invitation.

It was quiet on Reception at this time of night, and Ellie took advantage of the lull to catch up on some of the paperwork that seemed never-ending where running a hotel was concerned.

Her parents had run the hotel until two years ago, when her father had suffered a mild heart attack and been ordered to take it easy for a while—an opportunity her mother had taken to whisk him away to Spain to live in early retirement. Their parents had given the hotel equally to Beth and Ellie, but since taking over Ellie had realised exactly why the hotel had been such a strain on her parents; it was a twenty-four-hour-a-day job, and left little time for anything else. She—

'Good evening, Ellie,' greeted a huskily male voice. 'Do you ever get away from this place?'

The question so echoed the sentiments of her own thoughts that she wasn't able to maintain her usually bright smile as she looked up at Peter, their master chef, as he stood at the other side of the reception desk.

The restaurant was open to the public as well as to guests, and it was one part of the hotel that did make a profit. And justifiably so; Peter was a chef of a calibre Ellie had never met before, and had brought people into the restaurant from far and wide since he had taken over in the kitchen six months ago. She knew they were lucky to have found him and didn't question their good fortune too deeply—she just gave thanks for it every day. Without Peter's expertise as a chef she knew they would be in even more dire financial straits than they already were.

'Not as often as I would like, Peter,' she answered somewhat wistfully, her chin resting on her palm as she leant on the desk-top looking up at him; he was one of the few men she *could* look up to when she was wearing high-heeled shoes, as she was now—Peter was a little over six feet tall, a good-looking man in his late thirties.

He shook his head. 'I wish you would accept my invitation for the two of us to go out. I see by the rota that you're off tomorrow evening too...'

This was, as Peter had so rightly pointed out, far from the first time he had invited her out. It wasn't that she didn't find Peter's blond good looks attractive, because she did, very much so; she just didn't think it was a particularly good idea to go out with someone she was working with almost every day. It could be very uncomfortable for everyone if it didn't work out. And Peter really was an excellent chef...

Besides, she was hoping that tomorrow evening she and Beth would be dining with Daniel Thackery!

She gave Peter an apologetic smile. 'I already have an appointment tomorrow evening. I'm sorry.'

He grimaced, obviously in no hurry to leave. His shift was over for the evening and the restaurant would be closing shortly— only the lingering coffee-drinkers were left. 'Out of luck again,' he said teasingly. 'Who's the lucky man?'

He didn't know who he was himself yet, and she somehow doubted he would think of himself as 'lucky' when he did—although hopefully a sense of politeness towards James's wife would make him accept the invitation. 'No one you know.' She shrugged dismissively.

'Aha!' Peter looked interested now, leaning conspiratorially across the desk. 'A secret lover, hmm?' His brown eyes twinkled with mischief.

'Hardly!' Ellie chuckled softly. 'I don't have time for lovers—secret or otherwise—'

'Are there any messages for me?' interrupted a harshly cold voice.

Neither she nor Peter, she was sure, had been aware of anyone approaching the desk. But Ellie recognised that voice only too well; hadn't she listened to him earlier when he'd been talking to 'Darling' before making that telephone call to his fiancée? And she was sure, from the faintly disdainful expression on his face as he looked at the two of them, that he had overheard her ill-timed remark about lovers!

She turned to check the box for his suite, studiously hiding any awkwardness she might feel at his having heard her conversation with Peter. 'No messages, Mr Thackery,' she told him with a brightly professional smile, noticing the woman standing a short distance away watching the exchange uninterestedly—probably 'Darling', of the long, silky legs!

He nodded abruptly, his expression still grimly disapproving as he glanced briefly at Peter. 'I'll be in the bar if there are any—' He broke off abruptly as he was racked by a sudden sneeze. 'Damn it!' he muttered furiously, his gaze a fierce blue glare now.

Ellie maintained her smile of cool politeness. 'You seem to be starting a cold, Mr Thackery. I'm sure we have something you could take for that, if you—'

'I don't have a cold,' he cut in harshly. 'I'll be in the bar if there are any calls for me.' He gave an abrupt nod of dismissal before turning on his heel and striding off across the reception area to join the woman waiting near the entrance to the bar—a tall, blonde woman, her beautiful face animated as she put her hand through the crook of Daniel Thackery's arm.

If his fiancée called again he would be in the bar, Ellie guessed crossly. Well, she hoped none of them were expected to lie for this man; if Angela telephoned again Ellie had every intention of telling the other woman exactly where he was. Not who he was with, of course, but it would be up to Daniel Thackery to explain away his presence in the bar. She—

'I seem to know that man,' Peter said slowly as he gazed after Daniel Thackery with narrowed eyes.

Peter was a hotel employee, so there was no problem in revealing the identity of a guest to him. Besides, after her exploits in Daniel Thackery's suite earlier, who was she to preach about a guest's right to privacy?

'That's Daniel Thackery,' she told Peter flatly.

'*The* Daniel Thackery?' Peter said slowly.

Was he 'the' Daniel Thackery? He was known worldwide as a very successful businessman, with his restaurants in the capitals of the world frequented by the cream of society, so she supposed that, yes, he was 'the'!

'Yes,' she confirmed abruptly. The man under discussion had entered the bar with the beautiful blonde now, and Ellie turned her full attention back to Peter.

'I see.' He whistled softly through his teeth. 'What does a man like that want in a sleepy little place like this?'

What indeed? It was what Ellie wanted to know too. 'Anonymity, probably,' she snapped. 'If the woman he's with is anything to go by.' She grimaced her disapproval of the other woman.

Peter's brows rose. 'She looks rather beautiful to me.'

Oh, there was no doubting that the blonde was absolutely gorgeous to look at—tiny in height, with an hourglass figure, long legs and a youthfully beautiful face. But there was also no dismissing the fact that the man she was with was getting married next week—or that 'Darling' was well aware of Angela's existence!

'The two of them aren't married,' was all that Ellie could think of by way of explanation for her own bitchiness; after all, she could hardly admit to hearing of the existence of Daniel Thackery's fiancée while hiding in his wardrobe!

Peter grinned, leaning conspiratorially over the desk towards her. 'Signed themselves in as Mr and Mrs Smith, did they?' He gave her a teasing wink.

Ellie had to smile at that ludicrous wink. 'Sorry.' She gave a rueful smile. 'There's just something about that man that puts my hackles up.' That had to be an understatement; just being anywhere near that man seemed to set her teeth on edge!

Peter still smiled, straightening away from the desk. 'That isn't—or so we're led to believe by the newspapers—what women usually have to say about him!'

'Well, I'm not one of his usual women.' The tartness returned to her voice, her green eyes flashing. 'Anyway, he seems to prefer tiny blondes,' she added scornfully.

'Whereas I prefer tall redheads.' Peter looked across at her appreciatively. 'Sure I can't tempt you with dinner tomorrow evening?' he added wistfully, the subject of Daniel Thackery clearly forgotten.

At least, it had been forgotten by Peter. Ellie couldn't forget about him—because she hoped she and Beth would be dining with him tomorrow evening!

'I'll even cook for you,' Peter added persuasively. 'If you come to my apartment.'

The temptation of eating a meal Peter had cooked was one not many women would resist. But Ellie had other priorities for tomorrow evening.

'I'm really sorry, Peter,' she refused again with a regretful smile. 'I really am busy tomorrow night.' She hoped!

'I know when not to push it,' he accepted with a dismissive shrug. 'Another time. I had better be on my way,' he said with a brief glimpse at his wristwatch. 'My cat will be wondering if I've found myself a woman other than her!'

Ellie chuckled throatily. 'See you in a couple of days' time.'

He nodded. 'Have a good time tomorrow night. Whatever it is you're doing.' He gave her another suggestive wink before leaving.

Ellie shook her head, smiling fondly. He really was the most outrageous man, but she liked him anyway, found his light-hearted banter refreshing. It was a pity about tomorrow evening because if it hadn't been for this thing over Daniel Thackery she might just have accepted Peter's invitation...

'Could you arrange for an early-morning call tomorrow, please?' rasped the harsh voice that was becoming so familiar to Ellie—unfortunately so!

She turned slowly to look at Daniel Thackery as he glared across the desk at her. He had only gone through to the bar a few minutes ago; what—?

'An early-morning call,' he repeated impatiently as she blinked up at him uncomprehendingly. 'Do you think you could manage that?'

Colour darkened her cheeks at his sarcasm, and she bit her lip to stop herself returning an equally sarcastic reply. 'I'm sure I can,' she said tautly.

'At seven-thirty,' he nodded. 'And coffee,' he added tersely before he was racked by another sneeze.

Ellie automatically noted down the time of the early-morning call and the request for coffee.

'Coffee for one,' he corrected as he saw what she had written down on the pad in front of her, his mouth twisting with mocking amusement as Ellie looked up at him sharply. 'My guest has departed for the evening,' he explained drily as he saw Ellie's instinctive glance behind him for the diminutive blonde.

Ellie could have kicked herself for being so obvious. But she had assumed—incorrectly, it now seemed—that 'Darling' would be spending the night with him in his suite. But she wished she hadn't made what she had thought so obvious, hated that know-ingly mocking glint in those deep blue eyes.

'I only booked the suite for one guest,' he told her softly. 'Myself,' he added, before he gave yet another sneeze.

She was regathering her scattered wits now, forcing herself to meet his derisive stare with a cool green gaze. 'The suite is booked in its entirety, Mr Thackery,' she told him coolly. 'Regardless of the number of guests.'

'Really?' Dark brows rose. 'In that case—' his voice lowered huskily as he leant forward over the desk '—perhaps you would like to join me upstairs? For a nightcap?' he added lightly as he saw the shocked way her eyes widened.

First the blonde. Then his fiancée. Then the blonde again. And now her. He really was having a busy evening where women were concerned, wasn't he? Or was he...? Neither his fiancée nor the blonde was here, was she...?

Ellie smiled up at him with sweet insincerity. 'You seem to be developing a rather nasty cold, Mr Thackery.' She managed to keep her voice neutrally polite. 'I would suggest it might be more beneficial—to everyone concerned—if you snuggled down in bed with a cold-remedy or a hot toddy rather than a woman!' She met his gaze challengingly. Really, this man had an incredible nerve.

He appeared completely unruffled by her refusal. 'Permit *me* to know what is "beneficial" to me,' he dismissed arrogantly. 'And, as I told you earlier, I do not have a cold.' As if to prove him wrong he gave another sneeze. 'I would suggest, however,' he rasped once the sneeze had dispersed, 'that if you do decide to join me in my suite for a nightcap you wash off your perfume before joining me. I happen to be allergic to Sapphire,' he added with a grimace. 'You see—Ellie . . .' he said her name softly after looking at her name-tag attached to her blouse ' . . . it makes me sneeze.' He looked down at her unblinkingly now.

Ellie's mouth opened. And then closed. And then opened again. But no sound came out.

He had sneezed late this afternoon when she had booked him in. And earlier in his suite—he had been sneezing then too.

Because she had been hiding in his wardrobe wearing Sapphire!

Every time he came near her he started to sneeze. As he had in his bedroom earlier tonight—and even more so as he'd stood on the other side of the wardrobe door. Had he known she was there? *Did* he know?

He gave a dismissive shrug as the silence stretched between them—through pure shock on Ellie's part! 'I won't actually be going to bed for a while, so if you should change your mind about the nightcap... Or just feel in the mood for a chat,' he added—tauntingly, it seemed to Ellie. 'But don't forget about washing off the perfume before you come up,' he advised before strolling off in the direction of the lift.

Ellie stared after him, knowing her face was very pale. She was so stunned that she still hadn't been able to make so much as a movement when he turned

after stepping into the lift to give her a parting gesture
of his hand before the doors closed in front of him.

Had he known she was in his bedroom earlier? *Did
he know?*

CHAPTER TWO

'IT'S a nuisance that it's Peter's evening off.' Beth frowned as she battled to take the stone out of the centre of the avocado without actually damaging the fruit. 'We could have done with his expertise in the kitchen tonight if we're to soften Daniel Thackery up enough to get any information out of him!' She grimaced as the stone finally popped out of the fruit only to roll across the floor.

To Ellie's immense dismay Daniel Thackery had accepted Beth's invitation to dinner this evening. Beth had managed to speak to him this morning before he'd left for a business appointment, and he had been only too pleased, according to Beth, to accept dinner with an old friend. But after his parting comments to Ellie the evening before she really had no desire ever to see the man again. She was certain that if he didn't actually know for sure, then he at least suspected her presence in his suite the evening before—otherwise why would he have made those comments about her perfume and suggested a chat?

Her first instinct the night before, once she had recovered from the shock, had been to go up to his suite and brazen the situation out—at least find out what he did know. But then common sense had prevailed, and she had realised she would be playing into his hands by going anywhere near his suite again that evening; if she didn't go near him, he couldn't ask her any embarrassing questions.

But before she could tell Beth that she had changed her mind about inviting the man for dinner Beth had come and told her she had already asked him—and he had accepted!

'He ate in the restaurant yesterday evening,' Ellie told her sister distractedly. 'He knows how good a chef Peter is.'

'But even with the two of us making our best effort we're nowhere near as good,' Beth groaned, having retrieved the stone from the floor now and placed it in the bin.

Ellie shrugged, having been given the job of shelling the prawns to go with the avocado. 'Just ply him with lots of wine—that should mellow him,' she dismissed scathingly. 'Anyway, I told you I have to stand in on Reception this evening, so you're on your own with this dinner,' she announced with satisfaction. She had never been so relieved in her life to have had two people call in sick for this evening, one of them being their evening receptionist; she did not want to spend several hours sitting with Daniel Thackery trying to be polite to him, no matter what his reason for being in the area!

She no longer cared what his reason was; he couldn't buy their hotel if they weren't interested in selling. And they weren't! And Beth's interest in James was a private thing; her sister didn't need her presence at dinner to ask Daniel Thackery whether or not he had seen her husband recently.

'You don't have to go on Reception until ten o'clock,' Beth protested. 'Plenty of time for you to have dinner with us first.'

'That's true,' Ellie accepted grudgingly. 'But one of the bar staff is off sick too, so—'

'Send Doris in there,' Beth interrupted practically. 'She's done it before, so that shouldn't be a problem. And the two of us can turn back the beds in the rooms. We aren't that heavily booked, so it shouldn't take long.'

She sometimes wished her sister weren't so practical. Or so logically capable. But the two of them had been brought up in this hotel, had watched their parents' management of it for years, and they had learnt how to deal with staffing and other problems. And Beth's answer to the problem now was perfectly correct. It was just that Ellie didn't want to be present at the dinner!

She wanted to avoid Daniel Thackery for the rest of his stay—still had the uncomfortable feeling that he knew exactly where she had been the evening before. And, if he did, there was no way he was going to let something like that pass without further comment.

'Ellie, will you finish the prawns so that we can get on with preparing the chicken?' Beth impatiently interrupted her wandering thoughts. 'It's almost seven o'clock now, and if we have the beds to turn back...'

Which meant she had lost her argument about joining Beth and Daniel Thackery for dinner. Damn. But she really couldn't come up with another excuse not to join them—not without alerting Beth to the fact that she really didn't want to spend any more time in the man's company. There was just something about him, the wardrobe incident apart, that set her teeth on edge...

And, appreciative of the way her luck was going at the moment, she wasn't in the least surprised when Beth elected to do the beds on the second floor, leaving Ellie to deal with the first floor. Daniel Thackery's suite was on the first floor...

Taking all possible precautions against bumping into him accidentally, she rang up his suite first and received no answer. Nor did her loud knocking on the door of the suite. Good, he was still out. Although he was cutting it a bit fine if he intended joining them for dinner at eight o'clock; it was almost seven-thirty now...

He certainly wasn't an untidy man. In fact, looking around at the neatness of the suite, she acknowledged that it was difficult to tell whether it was occupied or not—no personal effects were lying around anywhere. But he was definitely still staying here; Ellie would have been the first to know if he had booked out. And the first to give thanks. He had been a disruptive influence on her life ever since he'd first booked in. And she had to sit down to dinner with the man in—oh, just over half an hour.

She would get this over with as quickly as possible and make good her escape; the last thing she wanted was Daniel Thackery returning to his suite while she was still there!

She had barely begun to turn back the bed when she heard the sound of a door opening behind her.

She turned sharply, her expression one of guilty dismay. Not that she had anything to feel guilty about tonight, but—

It hadn't been the bedroom door that had opened, but the adjoining bathroom door. Daniel Thackery must have just taken a bath or shower. His hair was still damp—his body completely naked!

Ellie just stared at him, hardly able to breathe. He— She— They— Oh, *God*...!

Daniel looked no more pleased to see her standing in his bedroom, apparently rooted to the spot, than she was to see him. A dark scowl marred his handsome features as he returned her stare. 'You again!' he snapped disgustedly.

She was still too shocked to react to that 'again', keeping her gaze riveted to his darkly scowling face after that first shocked recognition of his nakedness. There would be time later to remember the smoothly muscled contours of his body, his darkly tanned skin, the almost black hair that lightly covered his body. For now she had to concentrate on explaining herself—and then getting out of here!

'I did telephone and knock before coming in to your suite.' She rushed into breathless speech. 'There was no answer, so I—'

'I was taking a shower.' He drily stated the obvious, making no effort to cover up his nakedness. 'But the offer was for last night, not tonight!'

Her face suffused with colour as his meaning became clear. 'The maid wanted to turn back the bed—'

'Then why didn't she?' Dark brows rose over piercing blue eyes.

Why didn't he put some clothes on, instead of just standing there completely unconcerned with his nudity? *He* might be accustomed to being naked in front of women, but she certainly wasn't used to being in the same room with men who had nothing on. And who seemed completely unruffled by the fact!

'Because for this evening I am acting as the maid,' she bit out forcefully. 'Our usual maid is in the bar because we're short-staffed, and—'

'Never mind, Ellie,' Daniel interrupted in a bored voice. 'I get the picture. You—' He broke off with a frown as the telephone began to ring on the bedside table. 'It's like being stuck in the middle of a traffic junction! Get that, will you, while I put something on?' he said impatiently.

She was relieved that he was at last going to cover his nudity, but she was not his personal secretary. The fact that she was here at all was because of a set of circumstances she had no control over. She—

'Ellie!' he prompted again harshly as the telephone continued to ring and she made no effort to answer it. 'Just get it, will you?' he said wearily at her mutinous expression, turning away to open the wardrobe door and look through its contents for something to put on.

She snatched up the receiver. 'The Grafton Suite,' she barked automatically, keeping her gaze firmly averted from Daniel, not wanting to watch him as he dressed. It would be too intimate an action, and intimacy was definitely something to be avoided between herself and Daniel Thackery.

'Oh, good grief.' The female voice on the other end of the line sounded almost as impatient as Daniel had when the telephone had begun to ring seconds ago. 'I asked to be put through to Daniel Thackery's room, and instead I've been connected with another part of the hotel. Are you able to put this call back to Reception?' the woman continued briskly. 'Or will I have to call back and start again?'

She didn't exactly sound pleased at the prospect. 'Actually, you have been put through to Mr Thackery's suite,' Ellie answered while giving Daniel Thackery a beseeching look.

She was relieved to see that he was at least wearing a pair of black underpants now. Not that the brief garment made any difference to the intimacy of the situation. He might be wearing as much now as he would at a swimming pool or at the beach, but this wasn't either of those places—and the two of them were completely alone here in his bedroom. Except for his female telephone caller!

'But he—er—he can't come to the telephone just now,' she continued conversationally as Daniel Thackery made no move to take the receiver but continued to look through the wardrobe for his clothes for the evening. 'He—'

'What do you mean, "he can't come to the telephone just now"?' the woman cut in sharply. 'What—?'

'Thanks, Ellie.' Daniel at last took the receiver from her unresisting fingers, lifting it to his ear. 'I thought it must be you, Angela.' He spoke drily into the mouthpiece. 'A member of the hotel staff. Yes, a female member of the hotel staff,' he acknowledge, with a mocking look in Ellie's direction. 'How observant of you, Angela. No, I'm not up to anything,' he added hardily. 'Angela,' he said impatiently a couple of seconds later, 'will you stop giving me a damned day by day countdown to the wedding? I'm well aware of the fact that it's only ten days away!' he snapped harshly.

Wedding . . . Good God, yes—this man was getting married in ten days' time.

Ellie had been standing close to him, unable to take her eyes off the lean strength of his body, aware of the clean, male—unscented!—smell of him, all of her senses aware that he really was a very attractive man. But the realisation that he was talking to his fiancée on the telephone, to the woman he intended marrying next week, was enough to break the spell. She had to get out of here, had to—

'Where are you going?'

Ellie had almost reached the door, and escape, but she knew from the way Daniel had raised his voice that he was talking to her. She came to an abrupt halt, turning slowly to raise her gaze to meet his. Daniel was watching her from across the room with narrowed eyes, his hand over the mouthpiece of the telephone, his full attention on Ellie.

'Where are you going?' he repeated evenly. 'I thought you came in here to turn down the bed,' he reminded her mockingly, his blue eyes gleaming with humour now as he saw the almost desperate way she eyed her avenue of escape only feet away before turning back to look at the almost untouched bed beside him.

Her eyes flashed deeply green at his mockery. 'It's a courtesy thing only,' she snapped. 'I'm sure you're more than capable of dealing with it yourself!'

He eyed her challengingly. 'Surely it's what your employer pays you to do?'

Two bright spots of colour appeared on her cheeks. Who did he think—? A sudden realisation occurred to her: he didn't *know* she was co-owner of this hotel, appeared to have no idea she was Beth's sister. Probably because he didn't expect to see the owner of the hotel on the reception desk or in the rooms turning back the beds. But this was a small, family-run hotel, and she and Beth had always filled in wherever necessary.

And then another, more wicked thought occurred to her. If he didn't know she was Beth's older sister, then he didn't realise he was having dinner with her later this evening either...

'And I suppose you would tell her I've been lax in my duties,' she said in a disgruntled voice, deliberately keeping her head down as she moved to turn back the bed; if she had looked up at him at that moment he would have seen the laughter in her eyes— at his expense! 'And if I lose my job what will happen to the husband and seven children I have at home?' she added accusingly.

His mouth twisted. 'You're too young to have seven children!' he scorned disbelievingly.

Ellie met his gaze with steady innocence. 'I was a child bride.'

'You would have to have been,' he said drily. 'Are you really—?'

'Don't you have someone waiting to talk to you on the telephone?' Ellie reminded him lightly. 'And I have the rest of the rooms to see to.' She walked back to the bedroom door. 'I hope you enjoy the rest of your stay, Mr Thackery,' she told him dismissively as she prepared to leave.

'I'm sure I will,' he said slowly, his frown obvious in his voice.

Ellie didn't turn to look at him, making a dignified exit and no longer feeling at such a disadvantage where Daniel Thackery was concerned. Yes, he might have his suspicions about her presence in his room last night, but she had also been in his suite this evening, so if directly challenged she could always make the claim that it must have been the lingering smell of her perfume that had caused him to sneeze.

And she now had a certain advantage inasmuch as he didn't realise that she actually co-owned this hotel and that he was having dinner with her this evening. She didn't feel quite so awkward about the situation now. In fact, she was quite looking forward to the dinner now!

Beth eyed Ellie with a frown a short time later as she moved about the kitchen humming to herself as she put the finishing touches to the dessert. 'You seem to have cheered up since our conversation earlier,' she said suspiciously.

Ellie gave a dismissive shrug. 'I was a bit concerned about the staff problem. But it's all sorted out now, so we can relax for a while. Will you be OK here while I just go and change?'

'Fine,' Beth answered distractedly, still eyeing her uncertainly. 'But what's wrong with what you're wearing?'

She was still in the smart skirt and blouse she had been wearing to work in all day, and while she accepted that they were perfectly suitable to entertain in she wanted to be able to disconcert Daniel Thackery completely. And, looking and feeling her best, she felt sure she would be able to do that.

'I feel like changing,' she dismissed. 'I won't be long.'

Just long enough to freshen up and change into her little black dress—a figure-hugging sheath of a dress that finished just above her knees. Her legs were long and shapely, her hair she had washed that morning, so it swung silkily about her shoulders, and she added light make-up to her creamy complexion, red gloss to her lips. The overall effect was one of cool elegance.

Let's see what Mr Daniel Thackery thought now of the hotel receptionist-cum-maid who was also a child bride with seven children!

She could hear the murmur of voices in the sitting room as she approached—Beth seemed to have relaxed enough at least to engage in conversation with their guest. What was he going to think when Ellie joined them?

He turned frowningly when she opened the door to enter the room, that frown turning to puzzlement as he instantly recognised her. Well—he thought he recognised her; he obviously still had no idea she was Beth's sister. He rose slowly to his feet.

'Ellie!' Beth said with some relief. It was evident that she wasn't as relaxed in their guest's company as she had been trying to give the impression she was. 'Daniel is here,' she said unnecessarily.

Poor Beth—she wasn't at all happy, Ellie realised. Not that she exactly blamed her sister for feeling the way she obviously did, but the two of them were here now; surely together they could get through this evening?

'How nice,' she murmured with complete insincerity. 'I don't think the two of us have ever been introduced.' She moved forward into the room as she spoke, extending her hand in greeting. 'I'm Beth's sister, Ellie. And you are an old friend of James's.' She smiled at him as she spoke, and knew by the way his mouth tightened that he hadn't missed the slight barb in her tone when she'd said 'old' friend. Not that Daniel was in the least old— probably in his late thirties at the most—but she intended keeping him slightly off-balance if she could.

He clasped the hand she held out to him a little too tightly, painfully so for a few brief seconds, before slowly releasing it again. 'The two of you don't look in the least like sisters,' he murmured softly, his narrowed gaze taking in Ellie's appearance.

'We've fooled a lot of people with that over the years.' Beth smiled, starting to look more relaxed now that she was no longer alone with Daniel.

Beth had always been tiny and blonde, Ellie tall and red-haired—some people might have described her as statuesque—and when they'd been at school together it had disconcerted more than one person to find that Beth had a *big* big sister.

'I'll just bet you have,' Daniel said slowly, his narrowed gaze still on Ellie.

He looked very attractive himself in a dark blue suit and light blue shirt, with a conservatively patterned tie knotted meticulously at his throat. His hair had dried now, and was brushed back from his face, curling softly over the collar of his jacket.

'I'll just go and check on the chicken and put out our first course,' Beth put in brightly before she hurried from the room, obviously anxious to get the meal started.

There was silence once Beth had left the room, and Ellie met Daniel's gaze challengingly as he continued to look at her. She had no reason to feel embarrassed by the assumptions he had made earlier—but he did. Although she doubted embarrassment was something this man felt very often, no matter what the circumstances!

'What happened to the husband and seven children?' he finally said drily.

She gave a dismissive shrug. 'You know how it is— here today, gone tomorrow!' she said flippantly, green eyes alight with mockery.

'Is that a family trait?' he said hardily.

Ellie tilted her head questioningly, frowning slightly. 'Sorry...?'

Daniel shrugged. 'Your sister and James haven't been married very long, and yet they appear to be separated.'

Her mouth tightened at the implication. 'Surely that is between Beth and James?' she said pointedly; if by some chance he was here on James's behalf, she wanted to make it very plain what she thought of his interference.

He gave an abrupt nod. 'And you aren't the receptionist or the maid after all but the sister...' he said slowly.

Ellie looked at him sharply, not altogether sure she liked the way he'd said that either. 'Yes,' she answered almost defensively. 'I'm Beth's sister.'

'James has spoken of you,' Daniel murmured evenly.

She frowned, trying to read from his expression the meaning behind those words. For she felt sure there was one. But Daniel Thackery had made an art, it seemed, out of the enigmatic expression, and consequently, if there had been a double meaning behind the statement, she wasn't going to learn of it from looking at his face.

'How is my brother-in-law?' she returned just as guardedly; at least she might be able to find out the answer to the question that was most bothering Beth at the moment.

'The last time I saw James he was very well,' Daniel returned noncommittally, obviously having no intention of telling her exactly when that meeting had taken place.

It could have been months ago, before Beth and James's separation, for all Ellie knew. Although somehow she had an instinctive feeling that it hadn't been . . .

Ellie continued to meet Daniel's gaze for several seconds before finally turning away. 'Can I get you a drink while we're waiting?' she offered with cool politeness.

'Your sister has already provided me with a glass of wine, thank you.' He indicated the glass sitting on the coffee-table beside him. 'But I'll pour you a glass, if you would like one?' he offered mockingly.

It was almost as if he knew how much in need she felt of a soothing sip of wine! Probably he did. This man wasn't disconcerted for long; he had recovered fast from the surprise of realising she was Beth's sister.

'Oh, I couldn't possibly let you do that,' she refused with saccharine politeness. 'After all, you're our guest.'

'So it would appear,' he conceded drily. 'I notice, from my lack of sneezing, that you aren't wearing Sapphire this evening?'

Ellie eyed him warily. 'I do wear other perfumes,' she told him defensively. 'And in view of your remark concerning your allergy...' She shrugged with a casual dismissiveness she was far from feeling; she would rather not get into a discussion about the perfume that made him sneeze every time he went near someone wearing it! He might start to question her about the occasions when he had been sneezing during the last two days...!

His mouth twisted. 'That's very kind of you.'

'I can be kind, Mr Thackery—'

'Daniel, please,' he cut in smoothly, his gaze lightly mocking.

'Daniel,' she acknowledged distantly, moving to the dresser where Beth had left the tray containing the cooling bottle of white wine and the necessary glasses. 'Let me fill your glass up for you.' She smoothly crossed the room to pour the wine, hoping she had successfully diverted his attention away from that damned perfume; in view of the trouble it had almost caused her she never intended wearing it again.

Where on earth had Beth got to? She only had to check that the chicken hadn't gone dry and put the prepared avocados and prawns on the table; surely it couldn't be taking her this long just to do that?

'Cheers!' Daniel held up his glass once both glasses were filled. 'To an enjoyable dinner,' he toasted drily.

It was as if he knew very well that neither she nor Beth was actually looking forward to sharing this meal with him! Which he probably did. After all, Beth had run off like a scared rabbit and not returned, and Ellie knew she wasn't exactly being welcoming.

'Cheers,' she echoed abruptly, lightly touching her glass to his, pointedly not echoing his remark about 'an enjoyable dinner'.

Basically, she doubted it would be. There was an edge to her own conversation with Daniel, and Beth was hardly relaxed in his company either. What a wonderful evening this promised to be!

'Shall we sit down?' she invited as she smoothly lowered herself into one of the armchairs, crossing one knee over the other, her legs long and silky in the slightly dark tights.

Daniel sat opposite her, totally relaxed, still looking at her with narrowed eyes. 'I don't remember meeting you at the wedding,' he finally said thoughtfully—as if he would have remembered only too well if he *had* met her!

Which he probably would, Ellie conceded; the sparks seemed to have been flying between them since the moment they'd first met! 'Unfortunately I missed it because I wasn't very well,' she explained dismissively.

Dark brows rose. 'So unwell you couldn't make your only sister's wedding?'

Ellie sensed the censure in his tone and frowned. 'Yes,' she bit out tersely, having no intention of explaining to him, of all people, the reason she hadn't been able to attend Beth and James's wedding.

'That must have been rather upsetting for your sister.' He met her gaze challengingly. 'Although I believe your parents did come over from Spain for the wedding ...?' He arched dark brows.

'Yes,' she answered slowly. Of course her parents had come over for the wedding; they had stayed on for several weeks afterwards to help at the hotel too, what with Ellie in hospital and Beth away on her honeymoon.

Daniel nodded. 'I believe they left you and Beth in charge here after your father's illness?'

'Yes.' She replied warily this time; he had been busy doing his homework about them, hadn't he?

'So you and Beth must have come to rely on each other a lot over the last couple of years?' he ground out harshly.

She and Beth had always been close. At this precise moment Ellie felt as if she was under attack—and she wasn't exactly sure why. What difference did it make to this man whether or not she had been at Beth and James's wedding? What business was it of his anyway?

She shrugged. 'Beth understood why I couldn't be at the wedding.'

'Did she?'

Ellie's frown deepened at what she sensed to be open criticism now. 'I—'

'Dinner is served!' Beth announced as she came back into the room, smiling at them brightly, seeming to have no idea of the tension she had just walked in on.

Ellie had no real idea what it was about either. For some reason Daniel Thackery seemed to be openly challenging her. And it had nothing to do with her being in his suite—either yesterday evening or this evening.

So what was it all about...?

CHAPTER THREE

'WHAT a terrible evening!' Beth groaned, her face buried in her hands as she sat slumped in one of the armchairs.

'Terrible' was probably a slight exaggeration, in Ellie's estimation, but she had certainly spent better ones. Going to the dentist, something she particularly hated, was probably preferable to trying to get through an evening with a man who, although charmingly polite, none the less had still managed to give the impression of a closed clam that had no intention of being opened!

Both she and Beth had brought up the subject of James—and just as quickly had had the tables turned on them as Daniel had begun to tell them some anecdote or other about when the two men had been at school and then worked together. Very amusing, some of it, but not exactly what either she or Beth had wanted to hear.

And as for the subject of Daniel wanting to get into the hotel business . . . ! He had been even more close-mouthed about that—steering the conversation away from his own interest in it by asking them pointed questions about their own experiences in hotel management. Ellie had been suspicious about his interest in that at first, but as it had quickly become obvious that he was more interested in funny incidents that

48

had occurred than in their hotel in particular she had grown even more puzzled. If he was here on a fact-finding mission, either on James's behalf or with the intent of getting into the hotel business himself, he was hiding it very well.

As Ellie was sure he would do anyway. Daniel Thackery hadn't got to be the successful businessman he was today by being an open book when it came to his plans and ideas for the future.

'Not exactly a resounding success, I agree,' she told her sister now as she handed her a cup of coffee. 'But not a complete disaster either.'

Beth looked up at her with exasperation as she took the coffee-cup. 'We know nothing more about his reason for being here after spending four hours in the man's company than we did before we spoke to him!' She gazed glumly into her cup.

It *had* been four hours, as Ellie knew only too well herself. Daniel had seemed in no hurry to end the evening, still sitting chatting amiably with Beth in their sitting room when Ellie had returned from her hour and a half on Reception. She had thought he would be gone by the time she returned, but he had accepted another cup of coffee as he talked easily about the time he had recently spent in Russia.

It had been a fascinating subject, Ellie had to concede—but, as Beth had stated, of the man himself and his reasons for being here they had no more knowledge than they'd had before the evening had begun.

'But we have established contact—a friendly rapport,' she pointed out thoughtfully. 'It has to be easier after this to speak to the man again.'

Beth didn't look convinced. 'Do you really think so?'

Remembering Daniel as he had been this evening, she didn't, particularly! But she was trying to cheer Beth up. 'Why don't you try and contact James yourself...?'

'I couldn't!' Beth sat back, her body rigid, her face suddenly pale. 'That last argument—it was awful. He said things—'

'What sort of things?' Ellie prompted gently. Her sister had been very guarded about the argument she and James had had on that last evening when James had walked out, and out of deference to her sister's pain she hadn't pushed her before now to talk about it. But it was over a month now since James had walked out, and the longer this went on, the harder it was going to be for either of them to back down. If they did...

'Oh—just things.' Beth was avoiding her gaze.

'But—'

'I really don't want to talk about it, Ellie,' her sister snapped, her expression rebellious.

'Well, someone is going to have to,' she pointed out gently. 'Beth, you and James love each other; whatever is wrong, I'm sure the two of you could work it out,' she reasoned.

She liked her brother-in-law, thought he and Beth were good for each other, and she knew it would break Beth's heart if the two of them separated permanently. She had tried to stay out of this until now, hadn't thought it her business to interfere between husband and wife, but someone had got to do something soon to break this deadlock.

'No, we can't,' Beth insisted stubbornly.

She frowned. 'I don't see why not. Unless . . . There isn't another woman involved, is there?' The thought had only just come into her head. Which wasn't surprising; James had always seemed so much in love with her sister, it hadn't even occurred to her as a possibility before now.

Again Beth's gaze didn't quite meet hers. 'And if I were to tell you there was?'

Ellie shook her head. 'I think I would have trouble believing you,' she admitted honestly.

'Well, you would be wrong,' her sister told her tautly. 'There is another woman involved.'

'Beth, are you sure you haven't made a mistake?' she probed gently. 'James has always been such a one-woman man, I really can't see—'

'He's admitted it,' her sister cut in harshly, standing up abruptly. 'So there's nothing else to discuss on that subject.'

Ellie was stunned at James's admission, had never believed her brother-in-law would be capable of something so deceitful and hurtful to Beth. Another woman. It really hadn't even occurred to her.

She looked anxiously across at her sister. 'Beth—'

'I'm going to bed,' Beth interrupted. 'I'll see you in the morning.'

Ellie sat in the chair in the sitting room long after her sister had gone to bed. No wonder Beth had been so adamant about not contacting James this last month, claiming that if he wanted to talk he would have to come to her. After what he had done it had to be James who came to Beth. But at the same time she could see that her sister didn't want things to deteriorate to a state where all she and James talked about, when they did finally meet up again, was divorce. It was a very difficult situation. And not one that Ellie, at this moment in time, could see a way out of either.

She still couldn't believe that James had become involved with another woman; he had always seemed so much in love with Beth. They had even been talking about having a baby before their big argument a month ago.

Although with a man like Daniel Thackery as a friend and example—a man who was here with one woman while intending to marry another one next week—perhaps James's idea of a faithful relationship had become blighted by association!

It didn't help that the first person she saw, after leaving their private suite of rooms the next morning, was Daniel Thackery!

Even when not standing in on shifts she and Beth always tried to make themselves as visible as possible, both to the hotel staff and guests alike. Some of their guests had been coming here for years, remembered Ellie and Beth as children, and it was the personal touch that kept these people coming back year after year.

Although Daniel Thackery was one person Ellie hoped would never come back!

He was just leaving the dining room as she came through to the reception area; a meeting between the two of them was unavoidable—much as Ellie might want to avoid it! She had decided, during the course of the meal the evening before, that the sooner Daniel Thackery left, the better it would be for everyone. Personally she found his presence very disturbing, and his being here certainly wasn't doing Beth any good.

'Good morning, Ellie,' he greeted smoothly. He was wearing a dark business suit today, and a snowy white shirt with a grey tie neatly knotted at his throat.

'Mr Thackery,' she returned distantly. She was back in her more formal clothing this morning—a pencil slim black skirt and a pale peach blouse that made her shoulder-length hair appear more red than usual.

His mouth twisted mockingly. 'It was Daniel last night,' he reminded her huskily.

She was aware of the young girl on Reception looking up curiously as she heard that last remark, and felt her cheeks turn slightly pink. 'You were my sister's dinner guest,' she conceded stiffly, the implication being that she would not have been rude to anyone in those circumstances.

Dark brows rose over mocking blue eyes. 'But not yours?'

Certainly not hers; she hadn't liked him before, and last night certainly hadn't done anything to change that opinion. In fact, in the light of what Beth had told her about James's behaviour, and what she knew of Daniel Thackery's private life, the further this man stayed away from her the better.

Her mouth tightened. 'No,' she acknowledged tautly.

Daniel looked at her consideringly, not at all perturbed by her bluntness. 'Why don't you like me, Ellie?' he finally asked slowly. 'You don't even know me.' He shook his head curiously.

And she didn't want to either. The man had no morals. Was unscrupulous. Didn't—

'Or is it just enough that I'm a friend of James's?' he added harshly before she had time to formulate a reply that wouldn't sound too rude.

Her eyes widened, showing dark lashes surrounding deep green eyes. 'And what's that supposed to mean?' Her tone was indignant.

'I— Atishoo!' The sneeze was long-drawn-out, and Daniel's eyes had narrowed to steely slits when he finally recovered enough to look at her. 'You're wearing Sapphire again . . .' he said slowly.

Ellie met his gaze unwaveringly. 'Yes,' she confirmed unnecessarily. It was obvious she was wearing the perfume; Daniel had started to sneeze within minutes of meeting her again.

'Your consideration towards my allergy was only for the time I was your—I beg your pardon—your *sister's* dinner guest, hmm?' he prompted.

'I hardly expected to see you again first thing this morning,' she reasoned impatiently.

His mouth had tightened grimly. 'I only have to stand within ten feet of someone wearing the damned stuff and I— Atishoo!' He glared at her as he straightened. 'I start to sneeze!'

She knew that—hadn't she had the same effect on him even when standing inside a wardrobe wearing the 'damned stuff'? But it was one of her favourite perfumes, and she really had had no idea she would be seeing Daniel Thackery as soon as she came on duty. Not that it would have made any difference if she had. And he knew that!

'Then I will endeavour to make sure we don't meet for the rest of the day—the rest of your stay, in fact,' she told him dismissively, turning away.

The grip on her arm was not gentle as she was swung decisively back to face him; his expression was harshly angry now. 'What's made you so bitter and twisted, Ellie?' he ground out. 'A love affair gone wrong, that makes you belittle everyone else's chance at happiness? Is that why there's no time in your life for a lover, "secret or otherwise"?'

Her cheeks darkened with colour as he reminded her of the conversation he had overheard that first evening between herself and Peter. And how dared he call her 'bitter and twisted'? On what basis did he make such a sweeping judgement? Was it just because she made it obvious she didn't like him? Was every woman he met supposed to fall for the infallible Thackery charm? He was about as charming as a snake as far as she was concerned!

She wrenched out of his grasp. 'My private life is none of your business,' she told him tightly. 'I would put your own life in order before you attempt to make judgements on other people's!' She glared at him with flashing green eyes.

His gaze was narrowed thoughtfully. 'And what do you know about my private life?'

Her mouth twisted. 'That it isn't private enough!'

'Meaning?' he prompted softly, dangerously so.

Ellie gave an impatient sigh. 'You were at this hotel with one woman two evenings ago—'

'I wasn't "with" her. We were having dinner together—'

'And I answered the telephone yesterday evening to another woman—a woman called Angela,' she continued determinedly as he would have interrupted. 'A woman whose tone of voice gave the impression she had more than a casual relationship with you.'

'She does.' He nodded, his face grimly foreboding.

'So I gathered,' Ellie told him disgustedly. 'Two women in as many days seems slightly—excessive,' she added scathingly.

'No, Ellie,' he drawled hardily. 'Two women in *one* day is excessive!' He met her gaze challengingly.

Her head went back defensively. 'May I remind you that you also propositioned me two evenings ago?'

His mouth twisted. 'But you didn't take me up on it.'

'You still made the suggestion!' she reminded him sharply.

He shrugged. 'I didn't realise who you were then.'

Ellie stiffened at the insult she could hear in his tone. 'And what difference would it have made if you had?' she couldn't resist asking.

Daniel looked at her consideringly, from her trim black shoes to the blaze of her shoulder-length hair. 'A lot,' he finally answered. 'You aren't my type of woman, Ellie,' he continued harshly. 'I like my women to be soft and feminine and—'

'Clinging!' she added disgustedly, remembering the girlish femininity of 'Darling' that first evening. And how dared he imply that she wasn't 'soft and feminine'? He didn't even know her! As he claimed she didn't know him... She knew him well enough to know she didn't like him! Or his taste in women!

'Never clinging, Ellie,' he drawled dismissively. 'Heaven preserve me from that!'

Her mouth twisted contemptuously. 'You don't ask a lot, do you?' she scorned incredulously. 'Your perfect woman is soft and feminine but not clinging. What are your other requirements?'

He quirked one dark brow. 'Thinking of applying?'

'Certainly not!' she snapped. 'You no more meet my requirements in a man than I seem to meet yours in a woman!' She was breathing hard in her agitation. Really, this man was just too arrogant for words!

He gave an unconcerned shrug. 'Considering wimps are easy to find, I'm surprised you aren't already married.'

Ellie gave an involuntary gasp. 'Wimp', indeed; was that the sort of man he thought she wanted to spend her life with?

She had spent the majority of her adult life being strong and dependable, and knew now, at twenty-seven, that if she ever married she wanted someone who could be strong and dependable for her for a change. She certainly didn't want to marry a wimp!

'Your assumptions about my life are of little interest to me, Mr Thackery,' she told him frostily. 'As you are,' she added with deliberate insult; he had insulted her enough—why should she feel any reservations about doing the same?

'Really?' he challenged softly.

She frowned up at him for several minutes, inwardly annoyed that she had to do that; usually when wearing shoes with heels on, as she was today, she was on eye-level with most men. But not this one, Daniel being well over six feet in height. That knowledge only made her feel even more irritation towards him.

'Really,' she finally bit out scornfully.

He quirked dark brows. 'Is that in the nature of a challenge, Ellie?' he drawled.

'Certainly not!' she snapped impatiently. 'Now, as I suggested earlier in this conversation, it would probably be better—for all concerned!—if we endeavoured to stay out of each other's way for the rest of your stay.' Which she hoped wouldn't be for much longer. He had done nothing but cause chaos to her life since his arrival here!

His mouth twisted mockingly. 'That may be a little difficult,' he murmured slowly.

She gave him a sharply frowning look. 'Why?' she said warily.

Daniel shrugged. 'Because I just saw your sister in the dining room and she accepted my invitation for the two of you to join me for dinner this evening. In return for your hospitality towards me last night,' he added drily before Ellie could voice her protest.

Which she had certainly been about to do. Last night had been bad enough, but yet another evening spent in this man's company...! It was too much!

'I'm sure Beth was pleased to accept for herself.' She was sure of no such thing—was sure that Beth was no more comfortable in this man's company than she was. But her sister was the one who knew him, and as such she was also the one who would have to deal with him from now on. 'But I'm afraid I will have to pass; we can't both take the evening off,' she refused with as much politeness as the situation would allow.

'All work and no play—' Daniel drawled pointedly.

Angry colour darkened her cheeks at his intended insult. 'I "play", Mr Thackery,' she bit out tautly. 'I just happen to have a hotel to run too!'

'Beth had a solution to that,' he assured her smoothly. 'We can eat in the dining room here. That way you're both within call if needed.'

Damn!

She could see by the look of satisfaction on his face that he knew she wasn't pleased with the arrangement. Which just made her even more irritated.

She gave a bright, meaningless smile. 'That seems to be settled, then,' she bit out dismissively. 'Now, if you'll excuse me, I have work to do...' she told him pointedly, turning to leave.

'I'll look forward to seeing you later this evening,' Daniel called after her, the mockery clear in his voice—at least, to her.

* * *

Ellie went through the usual motions of work without really being aware of what she was doing, her fury towards Daniel Thackery an ever growing thing. She didn't doubt that he had deliberately talked to Beth about dinner this evening, was sure that he knew that if he had asked her directly she would have said no from the outset.

Who did he think he was? He seemed to be criticising every aspect of her life, from her dedication to her work to her possible future choice of a husband, while at the same time he was forcing her into situations she would rather have no part of. And that he *knew* she would rather have no part of; that was the most frustrating part of all this. Daniel Thackery was enjoying his apparent ability to manipulate her.

What was the saying? You can lead a horse to water... Well, Daniel might think he had got his way over dinner, and on the surface of it he had, but that didn't mean she had to be polite to him once she was there...

'I don't understand you,' Beth muttered irritably as they left their private quarters that evening to go to the dining room. 'When we were in private last night you got changed; tonight, when we're dining in front of all the guests, you decide not to bother!' She frowned her confusion.

Ellie shrugged dismissively. It was perfectly obvious to her—as she hoped it would be to Daniel—that tonight she had been coerced into a situation she wanted no part of. And, as such, she intended making no effort towards it either—was still wearing the blouse and skirt she had worked in during the day, with her hair secured in a slide at her nape.

Beth had made an effort herself this evening, wearing a fitted blue dress that exactly matched the colour of her eyes, complementing her slender figure and shoulder-length blonde hair.

'One of these evenings we'll both get it right!' her sister added ruefully.

There wasn't going to be another evening like this as far as Ellie was concerned; two evenings spent in Daniel Thackery's company was enough for anyone, she had decided.

'You look lovely,' she told Beth, without reference to her own businesslike appearance.

Her sister shrugged. 'I wouldn't want Daniel, if he should happen to see James, to tell him that I look as if I'm pining away for him!' she said stubbornly.

Even if she was! Her sister had lost weight over the last month, weight she could ill afford to lose, and there were dark circles under her eyes indicating that she obviously wasn't sleeping at night. But she did look pretty tonight—more animated than Ellie had seen her for some time—and Ellie was relieved to see that. She had been worried about Beth this past month, but had stuck to her decision that she shouldn't interfere in her sister's marriage break-up. Maybe now the shock had worn off Beth would start to open up to her and talk about the problems. Although if another woman *was* involved ...

'You look lovely,' she said again, to reassure her sister. 'Although it's slightly ridiculous being invited out to eat in our restaurant,' she added ruefully.

'That was Daniel's idea,' Beth dismissed.

Ellie frowned. 'But—'

'Ah, ladies.' The subject of their conversation stood up as they entered the reception area, obviously waiting for them. 'May I say how lovely you both look?' he added smoothly.

He could say it, and to some people it might even sound like a genuine compliment, but to Ellie it was just a mocking taunt. He knew damn well she had made no effort to dress up for this dinner, and to her heightened sensitivities he was just drawing attention to the fact by making the remark. Especially as he was wearing a black evening suit and snowy white shirt himself; his own and Beth's appearance made Ellie very much the odd one out.

Not that she particularly cared about that. This was purely a business dinner as far as she was concerned—dinner with a guest. A guest she didn't particularly care for...

Besides, she was still too perplexed by her conversation with Beth just before they'd joined Daniel to care that her own appearance wasn't exactly in keeping with the evening. Daniel had said it was Beth's idea to eat in the restaurant here, and yet Beth had just said it was *his* idea. And, knowing her sister as she did, she didn't need to wonder which one of them was telling the truth.

So why had Daniel lied about the decision to eat in the hotel restaurant...? Because she knew him well enough now to realise that he never said or did anything without there being a reason behind it!

'You look worried, Ellie.' He was watching her with amused blue eyes. 'Is anything wrong?'

She wasn't sure. She just knew she didn't trust this man. 'Not at all,' she answered smoothly. 'Shall we go through to the dining room?' she suggested distantly, still caught up in her own thoughts.

'You wouldn't like a drink first?' He indicated the bar.

Ellie met his gaze steadily. 'I don't think so. Unless you would care for one. But we do have an extensive wine list in the restaurant,' she added dismissively.

He nodded. 'So I noticed the other evening. In fact,' he continued while opening the door for them both to enter the restaurant, 'the dining room appears to be the hotel's main asset.'

Ellie stiffened at the word 'asset'. Could it really be true that he was here to look over their hotel with a view to making an offer for it?

'We recently had it decorated,' Beth answered as they all sat down.

'I wasn't referring to the decor,' Daniel drawled. 'Judging by the meal I had in here the other evening, your chef appears to be worth his weight in gold.'

'Peter?' Beth smiled, obviously starting to relax in Daniel's company. 'He certainly was a lucky find.' She nodded.

'How exactly did you find him?' Daniel asked interestedly. 'He appears to me to be the sort of chef who should be in an exclusive restaurant in London.'

'Do the people who live in London—the rich and successful ones, of course, the ones who can afford such *exclusivity*,' Ellie added derisively, 'have the monopoly on eating good food?'

He had annoyed her with the seemingly innocent remark, but at the same time she was puzzled by his interest in Peter. He certainly had been a wonderful find, but in truth it had been Peter who had found them, and not the other way round. The other man had just arrived at the hotel one day and asked if they might have a job for him. He had started out as the junior chef and very quickly taken over the whole kitchen—much to Ellie and Beth's relief! But that was none of Daniel's business . . .

'Not the monopoly, no,' Daniel answered slowly. 'I was thinking more of—Peter, was it? He could be earning really big money in London.'

Ellie's mouth twisted. 'Not everyone is money-orientated, Daniel,' she bit out dismissively.

'The implication being that I am?' He quirked dark brows at her.

She met his gaze unwaveringly. 'The implication being that— '

'Ah, here are the menus,' Beth interrupted with a certain amount of relief, smiling up at the waitress as she accepted her menu. 'Let's order a drink, shall we?' she suggested brightly. 'And then we can choose our food.'

Ellie knew exactly what her sister was doing, and, considering that they had the rest of the evening to get through, calming the situation down now was probably a good idea. If only Daniel didn't irritate and annoy her so much!

But she couldn't fault his choice of wine for their pre-dinner drink—as she couldn't fault the wines he selected to go with the rest of their meal once they had given the waitress their choices a few minutes later. Whatever else she thought of him, he knew good food and good wine. Unfortunately, she *did* think lots of other things about him too!

Amazingly she and Daniel had chosen to eat the same dishes—salmon soufflé followed by individual beef Wellingtons, both of which were delicious and simply melted in the mouth. As, Ellie was sure, did Beth's pâté followed by Dover sole.

'That was excellent!' Daniel announced appreciatively after eating the last morsel of beef Wellington on his plate. 'Could you ask the chef if I might have a word with him?' he requested of the waitress as she cleared their plates. 'You see, Ellie—' he turned back to her, humour glinting in his eyes '—we do have something in common. Maybe I do meet some of the requirements you have for a man, after all,' he added mischievously.

Choosing to eat the same food did not mean they had anything in common. And it certainly didn't mean he came anywhere near having the qualities she wanted in the man she might one day share her life with!

Her mouth twisted derisively. 'I doubt that very much.'

He grinned openly at her. 'You sound very sure of that.'

'Oh, I am.' She nodded firmly. 'I—' She broke off as she saw Peter making his way across the restaurant to their table, smiling up at him warmly as she remembered that he was here at Daniel's request.

Daniel had looked up at the other man too, standing up slowly with recognition dawning in his eyes. He gave Ellie a speculative look before turning back to the other man, obviously having realised that Peter was the man she had been talking to in Reception that first evening.

'Daniel Thackery.' He held his hand out in greeting to the other man. 'I just wanted to tell you how delicious the meal you prepared for us this evening was,' he added warmly.

'Peter Osborne,' the other man returned, shaking Daniel's hand. 'And I'm glad you enjoyed your meal.'

'Why don't you join us for a drink?' Daniel indicated the empty fourth chair at their table. 'I'm sure your two employers won't mind,' he added, with a teasing look in Ellie and Beth's direction.

Of course they didn't mind. But Ellie certainly hadn't appreciated that speculative look of Daniel's a few moments ago, obviously concerning her friendship with Peter. And that was all it was, even if Peter had invited her out on a few occasions—occasions on which she had had to say no.

'I'm still cooking, I'm afraid,' Peter refused regretfully. 'But it's been nice meeting you. And I hope you enjoy the rest of your meal. See you later, Ellie.' He smiled at her before leaving.

She was aware of Daniel watching her intently as he resumed his seat. She returned his gaze steadily, giving nothing away by her bland expression.

Just what did he think was going on between Peter and herself? Something, obviously. And it must also be perfectly obvious to him that Peter was far from being the wimp he had decided she wanted in her life!

'Has he been with you long?' Daniel asked softly, still looking at Ellie with narrowed eyes.

'About six months,' Beth answered with a shrug. 'The restaurant has been very popular since he took over as chef.'

'It would be,' Daniel nodded. 'It's still very odd that a chef of his calibre should remain—with all due respect, ladies!— in a small hotel like this. Maybe he has another reason for staying in the area?' Again he looked speculatively at Ellie.

She met his gaze. 'We really wouldn't know, Daniel,' she told him with cool dismissal, having no intention of confirming or denying his speculations about Peter and herself.

'No?' He didn't sound convinced, seeming to have drawn his own conclusions.

Completely erroneous ones as far as Ellie was concerned—and ones she was sure he wouldn't alter even if she were to deny them. Which she had no intention of doing. He could think what he liked about Peter and herself; it was of no interest to her.

'No,' she said uninterestedly. 'But I must say you seem inordinately interested in our chef. Anyone would think you were trying to steal him away from us,' she added mockingly.

'Not steal him, Ellie.' Daniel met her gaze unflinchingly. 'But I am hoping to make him an offer he can't refuse.'

Her mouth fell open as she stared at him incredulously. 'I beg your pardon?' she finally managed to utter in a strangulated voice.

He shrugged. 'Your chef's reputation has preceded him, and I'm here with the sole intent of trying to lure him away to work in one of my restaurants. It doesn't really matter which one. A man who can cook like that can take his pick of location as far as I'm concerned!' he added drily.

Ellie stared at him. And she knew Beth was doing the same, both of them speechless now.

Daniel returned their gaze, amusement glinting in his own eyes. 'Exactly why did you think I was here, ladies?' he prompted lightly.

CHAPTER FOUR

CERTAINLY not for the reason he was now claiming. He was here to lure Peter away from being chef in their restaurant! Which begged the question: How had he ever heard of Peter—or, more correctly, Peter's cooking—in the first place? But it did answer the question as to why Daniel had wanted to eat in the restaurant here tonight; he had wanted to make absolutely sure that Peter's ability was as good as he had initially thought it was before talking to the two of them about wanting to employ the other man himself!

Daniel sat back now, one brow raised mockingly at their obvious surprise at his statement. Well, what had he expected? Not only was he here to lure away their highly prized chef with promises of the pick of locations worldwide, but he also had had the arrogance to tell them so!

'I haven't spoken to Peter yet, of course,' Daniel went on at their continued lack of a verbal response. 'But I think, out of a sense of fairness, that I should tell you that I shall be doing so in the near future.'

Ellie's eyes sparkled deeply green as she glared across the width of the table at him. She was more than a little upset at the thought of losing Peter as their chef—and she had to face the fact that Peter would be insane to turn down an offer from someone like Daniel Thackery.

But they had been doing so well in the restaurant since Peter had taken over as chef—in fact it was his expertise in the kitchen, and consequently the success of the restaurant side of the hotel, that had been keeping them solvent for the last few months.

And now this man was here to take Peter away from them. And he would succeed too; of that Ellie had no doubt; Peter would never turn down an opportunity like this.

'That's very big of you, but since when did you have any ''sense of fairness''?' she finally snapped waspishly, losing the battle inside herself to contain her anger.

His eyes narrowed to steely slits. 'I wasn't aware we knew each other that well, Ellie,' he replied mildly—deceptively so, from the taut way his jaw was clenched. 'Or do you know something about me that I don't?'

She drew in a ragged breath. 'You—'

'Ellie, I don't think now is the time to discuss this,' Beth cut in quietly, looking about them pointedly—the restaurant was still quite full as diners lingered over their coffee after enjoying their meal. She turned back to Daniel. 'Perhaps we could meet in our office tomorrow morning to discuss this at—say, ten o'clock?' she suggested in a tightly controlled voice.

Ellie could see that her sister was just as furious about this unexpected development as she was, but practical Beth also had enough sense to realise that any conversation they had on the subject now was sure to become heated—on Ellie's side, at least—and that it was better left until they could talk in a more private place. Probably Beth was hoping that by tomorrow morning Ellie might have calmed down a little too!

Some hope! Ellie couldn't believe the nerve of this man. How dared he come here, masquerading as a guest? He was a friend of James's—How *had* he heard about Peter's ability as a chef? Surely James wouldn't have...? Perhaps Beth was right—they should talk about all this in the morning; at the moment her imagination was working overtime!

Daniel was watching the emotions flickering across her face, his own expression enigmatic now. 'Does that meet with your approval?' he asked pointedly.

Resentment flared in her eyes once more. 'Ten o'clock in the morning suits me just fine,' she bit out harshly, standing up abruptly. 'Now, if you will excuse me, we have a hotel to run.' She turned sharply on her heel and walked stiff-backed out of the room.

She kept up the dignified appearance until she reached the office at the side of the reception area—and then she allowed herself to slump back in the chair behind the desk there. If they lost the profit the restaurant was making for them due to Peter's talent...

She knew it wasn't a good idea to rely so heavily on one part of the hotel, but over the months it had been impossible not to do so. She realised now just how unwise they had been; even without Daniel Thackery's intervention it had been a big assumption to think that Peter, with all of his expertise, would stay with them for any amount of time. Judging by Daniel Thackery's accolade of the other man, they had been lucky to keep Peter with them for this long.

But that in no way excused the sneaky way Daniel Thackery had come here with the sole intention of stealing Peter away from them! He—

'I have a feeling,' drawled an all too familiar voice, 'that you would rather it were my neck you were wringing than that poor defenceless paperclip!'

Ellie had looked up sharply at the first sound of Daniel's voice, sitting up stiffly in the chair as she saw him standing in the open doorway across the room. She hadn't even heard the door open, let alone been aware that she was bending a paperclip so out of shape that it was almost unrecognisable as being such. Trust Daniel to know exactly what it was!

She dropped the mangled piece of metal into the bin next to the desk and heard it hit the bottom of it, her gaze never wavering from the arrogant-faced man who stood across the room. 'It says "Private" on the door,' she told him coldly.

He gave a shrug as he looked up at the notice. 'It also says "Please knock",' he drawled mockingly.

She raised auburn brows. 'Which you didn't!' Her hands were clenched so tightly together on the desk-top now that her knuckles showed white.

He came fully into the room, closing the door decisively behind him. 'I didn't what?' He strolled over to sit on the side of the desk.

Ellie drew in a deep, controlling breath. 'Knock!' she ground out harshly. He knew damn well what she had meant; he was just being bloody-minded now. And she wished he hadn't positioned himself so that he was looking down at her; it made her feel at a distinct disadvantage!

He raised dark brows. 'Didn't I?' he returned mildly.

'You know you didn't!' Ellie was having trouble containing her agitation. What she really wanted to do was wipe that self-satisfied smile off his arrogantly handsome face!

He gave a dismissive shrug. 'Surely it's irrelevant whether I did or I didn't; the request implies that this room isn't completely private—that guests are welcome.'

After they knocked—and this man wasn't 'welcome' in here even then. Not when she was in it! 'Our appointment is for ten o'clock in the morning, Mr Thackery,' she reminded him tautly.

His mouth quirked. 'So it's back to Mr Thackery, is it?' he drawled derisively. 'Sour grapes, Ellie, because of my intentions towards your chef? Haven't you heard the saying that all's fair in business?'

She looked up at him unflinchingly. 'I thought that was in love and war?' she bit out abruptly.

'I have a feeling that being in love with you might feel a little like being in war,' he murmured slowly, suddenly seeming far too close for Ellie's comfort, leaning towards her as he made the provocative statement. 'But maybe the battle would be worth winning,' he added with soft speculation.

Heated colour darkened her cheeks as his gaze roamed slowly over her face and body. 'You'll never know!' She stood up, moving abruptly away from him.

Daniel sat back, watching her with narrowed blue eyes. 'Never make sweeping statements, Ellie; they very often come back to laugh in your face,' he said drily.

She gave him a scathing glance, more self-assured now that she had put some distance between them. 'Not this one!' she scorned confidently.

'No?' Daniel stood up too, suddenly making the room seem much smaller.

'No!' Ellie faced him defiantly.

Which, she acknowledged as he walked slowly towards her, was perhaps not the right thing to do with this man; she doubted he had ever backed down from a direct challenge in his life! But she couldn't back down either; there was something about Daniel Thackery that brought out the stubborn streak in her.

He stood directly in front of her now, forcing Ellie to tilt her head back so that she could look up into his face. He was so close that she could see the specks of navy in already deep blue eyes, and his lashes, dark and silky—altogether too long and luxuriant to belong to a man.

His hand moved up to touch the confined hair at her nape. 'It's a sin to do this with hair as beautiful as yours,' he murmured throatily, deftly removing the tortoiseshell clip there, loosening the fiery red hair out onto her shoulders. 'That's better,' he added with satisfaction, his gaze admiring again now.

'Daniel—'

'Perhaps it's better if we don't talk, Ellie,' he said throatily. 'Let's see if we communicate better in another way.'

Ellie barely had time to digest his words—and understand their full meaning—before his head lowered and his mouth laid claim to hers.

Her initial response was one of rejection. How dared he? But as she struggled for release his arms tightened about her, and as she tried to free her mouth from its captivity one of his hands moved back to the nape of her neck, holding her head firmly in place. And making escape impossible!

His plundering mouth took on none of the savagery she had been expecting, but instead sipped and tasted from her lips, and she felt her resistance weakening, a warmth spreading through her body, a hitherto unknown yearning deep inside her. What...?

'Open your lips, Ellie,' Daniel murmured, slightly raising his mouth.

She swallowed hard, her eyes wide and apprehensive. 'I—'

'I want to be inside you, Ellie,' he murmured huskily.

The warmth became a burning heat at the intimacy of his words, and her gasp was one of anticipation. Daniel took advantage of her parted lips to claim them once again, his tongue hot and moist as it ran lightly over her lips before plunging deep inside her mouth.

It was like being possessed—her body curved intimately into his, her legs feeling weak, her arms up about his neck now, to stop herself from falling. Every part of her was moulded to the warmth of his body— his thighs were hard and demanding against her, and his tongue was plundering inside her mouth with a rhythm that brought liquid heat to her veins.

Ellie had never been kissed like this in her life before, had never known this wild need for something more, something deeper, something—

She wanted him to sweep her up into his arms, lay her down on the floor and make love to her fully. Wanted to know the full strength of this passion that had sprung up between them so suddenly and so completely that she couldn't think, could only feel—her hands caressing the hardness of his back now beneath the warmth of his jacket, her own silken legs entangled with the long, lean strength of his.

'God almighty, Ellie!' He raised his head to look down at her with eyes slightly unfocused with desire. 'What the hell are you doing to me?'

'Me?' She gasped her indignation. 'I—'

'No, don't start fighting me again,' he pleaded wearily, the dampness of his forehead resting against hers, his breath warm on her face as he still held her body moulded against his. 'The absolute madness of this is that I want to lay you down here on the floor and make love to you until both of us are too weak to move!' he groaned self-derisively.

His words so echoed her own thoughts of a few minutes ago that her cheeks flushed anew. He was right—this was madness; they didn't even like each other!

'Ellie, don't!' he protested gruffly as she would have struggled to be free once again, his arms holding her tightly against him. 'The only thing wrong with that is that we could have chosen somewhere slightly more—dare I say it?—' he gave a rueful grimace '—private than this to realise we want each other!'

They didn't want each other! Oh, they had responded to each other a few minutes ago—she couldn't deny that—but emotions had been running high anyway; what had happened just now was just an accumulation of circumstances—

'What thoughts are going on inside that beautiful head of yours now?' Daniel looked down at her frowningly.

Ellie pulled away from him, and this time—thankfully!—he offered no resistance, watching her with narrowed eyes. 'I'm not beautiful, Daniel. Remember, I'm "bitter and twisted",' she reminded him scathingly.

What on earth had she been doing a few minutes ago? How could she have responded so wantonly—to this man of all men?

His mouth thinned. 'Is that what just now was all about? Were you trying to prove a point?' he rasped harshly. 'If you were, you made a damned good job of it. Perhaps I finally have my answer as to why Osborne is wasting his talent in a small hotel like this one!'

'What do you mean?' she gasped, moving completely away from him until the two of them were facing each other angrily across the room.

His mouth twisted scornfully. 'I'm sure you know exactly what I mean,' he dismissed disgustedly. 'There must be easier ways to keep your staff, Ellie—no matter how good they are—than to sleep with them!'

Fury flamed in her eyes. 'You bas—'

'Ellie, I think we should—' Whatever it was that Beth thought they should do she obviously changed her mind about saying so when she saw that her sister wasn't alone in the office, frowning as she stood in the doorway looking at the two of them glaring furiously at each other. 'Ellie?' she finally prompted tentatively. 'I thought we were all going to meet here at ten o'clock in the morning?' She looked questioningly at Daniel when she received no reply from Ellie.

'Mr Thackery had other ideas,' Ellie finally answered her sister, but her gaze was still fixed contemptuously on Daniel. 'Completely different ideas,' she added challengingly, her hair in wild disarray about her shoulders—a circumstance her sister must be wondering about, she was sure.

He gave a dismissive shrug. 'They can wait.' He more than met her challenge. 'In the meantime, I suggest that neither of you—'

'I don't believe you are in a position to advise either of us to do anything!' Ellie cut in, incredulous at his continued arrogance.

'That neither of you mentions this matter to Osborne,' he continued with grim determination.

'Considering it's his future we're talking about, I think that *request*—' she emphasised the last word '—is not only arrogant, it's ridiculous!'

Daniel looked completely unperturbed by the vehemence of her outburst. 'Nevertheless, this is a business matter, and until we have it completely clear in our own minds exactly what I'm proposing I don't believe it serves any purpose to tell Osborne about it just yet.'

Ellie gave him a scornful look. 'Could it be that you don't want Peter to know just how keen you are to get him for one of your restaurants?' she taunted.

Daniel gave her a coldly quelling glance. 'I've told you, the man can more or less name his own price—'

'But you don't want *him* to know that!' she scoffed.

His gaze turned to ice as he arched one dark brow, and it remained on her unwaveringly for several long seconds before he turned abruptly to Beth.

'You seem to be the more level-headed one in the family.' His tone of voice softened noticeably as he spoke to Beth. 'Perhaps hot-headedness goes along with the fiery hair,' he added dismissively. 'Whatever—' he shrugged '—from a business point of view, I believe it would be more sensible if we put off discussing this matter any further—with anyone— until after the three of us have met tomorrow.'

Beth just looked puzzled, shaking her head. 'I actually agree with Ellie on this. I really can't see what difference it makes whether Peter knows now or in the morning; you seem pretty determined to take him away from us.'

Daniel frowned. 'I can understand why Ellie is taking this so personally, but I don't understand why you should be too.' His frown deepened thoughtfully as he continued to look at Beth. 'Unless—'

'Forget it, Daniel,' Ellie snapped, knowing exactly in what direction his thoughts were running—and, no matter what James's behaviour might have been over the last year, she knew for certain that Beth had remained completely faithful to her husband; she certainly had no romantic interest in Peter. As Ellie herself didn't, no matter what Daniel might think to the contrary! 'That idea is a non-starter!' she added warningly.

His mouth twisted mockingly. 'And you would know,' he accepted drily. 'Do you think you might manage to restrain yourself from any pillow-talk tonight, or should we have our conversation now?' he added derisively.

She drew in a deep, controlling breath. 'I think I'm managing to "restrain" myself very well so far,' she told him pointedly, having to clasp her hands together to resist the impulse she had to smack that derisive arrogance off his face. 'I should be able to do so for another few hours,' she bit out tautly.

'Very well, then, ladies.' He gave a dismissive nod of the head. 'I'll see you both in the morning.'

'Goodnight, Daniel.'

Beth was the one to answer him before he strode out of the room. Ellie couldn't have spoken another word to him if she had tried—well, not a polite one anyway. There were plenty of impolite ones she could have said!

'Ellie—'

'Don't, Beth,' she told her sister pleadingly, reaction starting to set in now, her legs feeling weak as she made her way over to the chair behind the desk to sit down.

She put her hands over her face, closing her eyes, breathing deeply. It was difficult to believe that she had so lost control—in Daniel Thackery's arms, of all people's. And to make things worse she couldn't even remember feeling that way with anyone else before...!

Oh, she had had the usual romantic forays in her teens and early twenties, but after that she had become much more 'choosy', as her mother put it, and was of an age now where she knew what sort of man she wanted to share her life and was not willing to settle for anything less. And Daniel Thackery, with his selfish code and lack of morality, was definitely less. He was certainly nothing like the man she hoped to spend the rest of her life with!

Then why had she responded to him so wantonly? What was it about Daniel that had so affected her that she had completely forgotten their surroundings—completely forgotten that she didn't even like him?

She didn't have the answer!

She dropped her hands down from in front of her, looking across at her sister, knowing that her eyes must look huge in the paleness of her face. She swallowed hard, not knowing what to say to Beth about what had just so obviously taken place between herself and Daniel—but knowing she had to say something.

'Oh, Ellie!' her sister choked. 'You look just like I did the night I met James!'

If she had been pale before, then Ellie knew that her face had now gone ghostly white. 'What do you mean?' she managed to gasp between stiff lips.

Beth crossed the room to stand beside her, putting her arm comfortingly about Ellie's shoulders. 'I knew it had to happen one day.' She shook her head. 'We Thompson women all do it, don't we?' She shook her head again. 'Look at Mummy—she fell for Daddy the moment she met him and they've been happy ever since. I did the same thing with James,' she added wistfully. 'One look, and that was me gone. We all seem to fall hard and fast—and just once in a lifetime. I don't know—'

'Beth, will you just stop there?' Ellie cut in firmly, standing up abruptly. 'You and Mummy may have fallen in love like that, but I hope you aren't suggesting I've just done the same thing? And with Daniel Thackery of all people!' she added scathingly.

Her sister watched Ellie consideringly as she began to pace the room in restless movements. 'Haven't you?' she prompted softly.

'Don't be ridiculous!' she scorned unhesitatingly. She might not have an explanation herself for what had just happened between herself and Daniel, but she was absolutely certain it wasn't what Beth was suggesting! Fall in love with Daniel Thackery? She would be safer falling in love with a rattlesnake—at least she would hear that and be aware of the imminent danger!

Beth frowned her puzzlement. 'But you and he were— The two of you had obviously been— Well, you know what I mean!' she concluded pointedly.

'Of course I know what you mean,' Ellie dismissed impatiently. 'But Daniel Thackery is a man who seems to have to try and seduce every single female of a certain age that he comes into contact with.'

'I don't think so.' Her sister slowly shook her head. 'James has always said that Daniel rarely gets involved with women, and even when he does it isn't

for very long. Daniel's reason for that, apparently, is
that he says he'll know the perfect woman for him
when he meets her, and until he does he isn't interested
in fleeting affairs that leave both parties feeling used.'

As Ellie now felt used. What other explanation
could there possibly be for Daniel's behaviour? The
man was getting married next week!

Beth grimaced. 'James told him he's looking for a
woman who doesn't exist.'

Ellie didn't want to hear what her brother-in-law
had advised his friend about his love-life, and she certainly didn't want to know anything about it herself.
She already knew all she needed to know about Daniel
Thackery!

'Well, it appears that he's actually found her,' she
said scornfully, though his attitude on the telephone
towards his fiancée had been more impatient than
lover-like. 'Because he's getting married next week!'

Beth blinked. 'Daniel is?'

She gave her sister an irritated look. 'That *is* who
we were talking about, Beth.'

'Yes. But . . .' Beth frowned. 'James didn't say anything about Daniel getting married.'

'Please don't take this the wrong way, Beth—' she
gave her sister a regretful grimace '—but it's some
time since you last spoke to James. And a lot can
happen in a month.' Look what had almost happened
to her in the matter of a few minutes!

'I suppose so,' her sister accepted slowly. 'Still, it's
a bit odd that Daniel is here—if, as you say, the
wedding is next week.'

'Oh, it is,' Ellie assured her with certainty. 'And for my part I think we've discussed Daniel Thackery enough for one evening.' She had enough thinking to do about him before she saw him again tomorrow, without having to actually talk about him too! 'It's this problem over Peter that most concerns me at the moment.' She frowned. 'If we lose him...' She grimaced pointedly.

'Hmm.' Beth nodded. 'There's always the possibility that Peter won't actually want to go... No,' she acknowledged ruefully at Ellie's sceptical look. 'He would be very silly to turn down an opportunity like this one,' she agreed heavily. 'I would love to know how Daniel came to hear of Peter in the first place.' She sighed.

Ellie didn't think that now was the time to voice her own possible theory about that. After all, she didn't actually *know* it had been James, and there was no point in making things more strained than they already were between Beth and her husband. Although she really couldn't think of any other way that Daniel could have heard about Peter...

'The fact is, he did,' Ellie dismissed briskly. 'And now we have to try and find some way to deal with it.'

Although she still had no idea how. They had been so reliant on the restaurant side of the business—stupidly so, she now acknowledged. Nevertheless, it was a fact that they were going to have a struggle to hold onto the hotel at all without the profits from the restaurant. Maybe they would have been better off if Daniel *had* wanted to buy the hotel after all...

CHAPTER FIVE

THE next morning Ellie was no nearer to coming to any conclusions about her uncharacteristic behaviour with Daniel than she had been the night before. But one thing she did know: she certainly didn't accept Beth's possible explanation for it. There was no way she could ever fall in love with a man like Daniel Thackery!

It was true about their mother and Beth—her parents had taken one look at each other and known they wanted to spend the rest of their lives together, and when their father had become ill two years ago their mother hadn't hesitated to go with him to the warmer climate his health now required. And Beth had reacted just as strongly to James when she'd first met him—and she remained in love with him, no matter what might have gone wrong in their marriage now. But to suggest that Ellie might feel the same way about Daniel . . .! Ridiculous!

'Why so despondent?' prompted a gently concerned voice. 'It can't be that bad, Ellie,' Peter cajoled. 'Nothing ever is when you really think about it.'

Ellie had been on her way to Reception before the dreaded meeting with Daniel at ten o'clock. She smiled warmly at Peter. 'I'll take your word for that,' she returned lightly. 'Breakfasts all finished?'

He nodded. 'Anything that needed cooking. Do you have time for a quick coffee before I go?'

Peter always disappeared for the couple of hours he had spare between breakfast and lunch—to go home and feed his cat, Ellie assumed. She didn't really know that much about Peter's private life—except that he had been gently trying to invite her into it over the last few months.

She glanced at her watch; she had twenty more minutes before the ten o'clock meeting, and there was absolutely no reason why she shouldn't spend them having coffee with Peter. No matter what Daniel Thackery might think to the contrary.

She nodded. 'But I have to be free by ten o'clock,' she explained ruefully. What on earth Peter would think if he knew that her ten o'clock appointment was to talk about him she couldn't imagine.

'Suits me,' he accepted. 'I have to be away from here by then anyway.'

They strolled back into the dining room to sit at an empty table by the window, and Ellie glanced around them as the waitress poured their coffee. The first person she saw was Daniel, his eyes glacial as he returned her gaze, having taken in everything about her businesslike appearance in that one condemning glance.

Damn!

It was obvious what he was thinking. But why shouldn't she have coffee with Peter? She had no intention of discussing Daniel's proposition with him. She accepted that Daniel couldn't know that, but then he shouldn't jump to conclusions.

She turned pointedly away, smiling warmly at Peter. 'It's nice to have this opportunity to talk to you. Are you still liking living in the area?' There was nothing to say she couldn't ascertain just how happy—or not—Peter was working here.

He nodded. 'It's a warm, friendly place. It's a pity James and Beth seem to be having problems at the moment, but I'm sure they'll work things out. People who love each other usually do. Besides, I miss the occasional pint I used to have with him in the bar,' he added with a grin.

'Have you heard from him?' Ellie frowned. It seemed hard to imagine that her brother-in-law hadn't made contact with any of his friends since he'd left.

'Not at all,' Peter dismissed easily. 'But I presume he'll be back—once he and Beth have sorted things out.'

'I hope so,' she said with feeling.

'I see our prestigious guest is still with us,' Peter remarked curiously, nodding in Daniel Thackery's direction when Ellie looked up at him questioningly.

'Yes,' she confirmed abruptly, turning sharply away as Daniel looked at her with narrowed eyes; he seemed to be making no effort to leave the dining room himself and was in the process of accepting another cup of coffee from the waitress. Just what exactly did he think she was going to do that he had to sit there watching her?

'Successful chap,' Peter said uninterestedly.

Ellie looked at him curiously. 'Doesn't success interest you, Peter?'

He shrugged. 'Only as much as the next man. No,' he added thoughtfully, 'probably not as much as the next man. There are more important things. But, as I said earlier, nothing is so important that it can't be worked through. And the thing about success is there's only one way to go once you reach the top.'

She gave a light laugh. 'I've never thought of it in quite that way before.'

Peter gave a rueful glance. 'I'm probably being over-simplistic by taking that view,' he acknowledged self-derisively. 'I think what I'm trying to say is that success doesn't necessarily bring you happiness.'

That was probably true; there could be no doubting Daniel Thackery's success in the business world, but he seemed far from happy in his personal life—the evidence of other women in his life when he intended getting married next week was surely an indication of that.

'What makes you happy in life, Peter?' she prompted, determinedly putting Daniel Thackery from her thoughts. It was a little more difficult to put him completely from her mind, however, when she could feel the coldness of his gaze boring into her from across the room.

He gave a lop-sided grin. 'Is this a trick question?'

'Of course not,' she denied laughingly. 'I'm just interested; we've just never really had time to talk like this before.'

'That's because you keep turning down my invitations,' he returned teasingly. 'I could have spent a whole evening boring you with my observations on life, instead of just twenty minutes!'

'You aren't boring me at all,' she assured him lightly. 'I have to admit I've wondered what a talented man like you is doing in a small place like this, but I think with your remarks about success you've just partially satisfied my curiosity.'

'Only partially?' Peter prompted.

'Hmm,' she returned, looking at him thoughtfully. He was a man in his late thirties, good-looking, obviously single, and with a talent as a chef that surpassed the majority; there had to be more to his being here than just a disillusionment with success. 'Why here, Peter? What on earth made you choose to come to Bramforth?'

He took a sip of his coffee, putting his cup back down on the saucer before answering. 'It's a long story, Ellie,' he finally answered slowly. 'I would probably need a whole evening to tell you.' He looked at her challengingly, brows quirked teasingly.

Ellie returned his smile. 'I think I've just talked myself into that one!' she acknowledged ruefully.

He looked surprised. 'Does that mean you've finally agreed to have dinner with me one evening?'

'It does.' She nodded, glancing at her watch. 'Could we talk about this again later? I'll have to go for this appointment.' No doubt Daniel would have plenty to say when they met up in the office; she would rather not give him anything else to complain about.

'Fine.' Peter stood up to pull back her chair. 'Don't forget,' he warned her softly as she turned to leave.

Daniel stood up as she approached the doorway, falling into step beside her. 'You couldn't resist it, could you?' he said hardily when, after several seconds, she made no effort to say anything to him.

Ellie was relieved that the first time they had seen each other again after last night she had been with someone else. She hadn't been looking forward to meeting up with him again, and, as she was always finding with this man, attack was definitely the best form of defence!

'I take it you're referring to my conversation with Peter?' She arched dark auburn brows at him.

'Of course I damn—' Daniel broke off abruptly, drawing in a controlling breath. 'I thought we had agreed you wouldn't talk to your boyfriend just yet about my job proposal?'

Ellie gave him a scathing glance, continuing to walk purposefully towards the office. 'Your statement appears to be inaccurate on two counts,' she told him coolly. 'Peter isn't my boyfriend,' she bit out coldly as he raised questioning brows, 'and I haven't discussed you with him at all.' Their mention of the level of this man's success didn't count! 'I have better things to do with my time than discuss you with anyone!' she added caustically.

'You—'

'Hello, you two,' Beth greeted brightly as Ellie entered the office ahead of Daniel. 'Have you started without me?'

Ellie had no reason to start or end *anything* with this man—with or without Beth! 'No,' she answered shortly. 'Shall we get this over with?' she asked Daniel abruptly. 'Beth and I have a hotel to run.'

Daniel took his time about answering, folding his lean length down into one of the chairs. He was dressed in a business suit and snowy white shirt, a Paisley tie knotted neatly at his throat. Ellie didn't need his formal attire to tell her this was a purely business meeting; the last thing this man was—or ever could be!—was a friend.

'And a chef you don't want to lose,' Daniel finally drawled.

Ellie shrugged, making no effort to sit down herself, knowing from experience that she felt at too much of a disadvantage with this man when she did. 'I still feel any conversation between the three of us is a waste of time—it will be Peter's decision whether or not he accepts your offer.' And after her earlier conversation with him about his views on success she was no longer sure that Peter would be interested in what Daniel was offering.

'I'm aware of that. But I wanted to make it plain to the two of you that I don't intend stealing your chef without giving you time to find a replacement. I'm aware that with a man of Peter's calibre,' Daniel continued firmly as Beth would have protested, 'that will be difficult to do. But, nevertheless, I don't intend just leaving you in the lurch here. A three-month period during which you look around for someone else should be acceptable to everyone, and—'

'Daniel,' Ellie cut in firmly. 'Until you have spoken to Peter, none of us knows whether or not that is really going to be necessary.'

He looked at her with narrowed eyes. 'I wanted to get things clear between us before approaching him.'

Her head went back derisively. 'I think Beth and I are the last ones to have any say in this, don't you?'

He gave her an impatient look. 'I think you are being unreasonable about this. I didn't *have* to tell you my intentions where Osborne is concerned at all!'

She met his gaze unflinchingly. 'Then why did you?'

'Politeness,' he bit out harshly. 'That sense of fairness I told you about last night. And I'm sure the last thing Osborne would feel comfortable with would be leaving here under a cloud. Taking what you want at a cost to someone else is not a very good way to conduct your life.'

Ellie stared at him. She couldn't help it. The statement he had just made was positively the last thing she would have expected from someone like him.

'As I'm sure Osborne is only too aware,' Daniel added drily.

But not necessarily him, Ellie realised derisively. For a moment, a very brief moment, she had thought that perhaps she had been wrong about Daniel's cut-throat attitude to life. How ridiculous!

'I'm sure neither Ellie nor I would want to stand in Peter's way, Daniel.' Beth was the one to answer him. 'But if what you're really talking about is the fact that we don't seem to be pleased about this that's another matter altogether. Of course we aren't pleased—we would be lying if we said otherwise,' she dismissed impatiently. 'The last thing we want is to lose Peter, but it will be his choice.'

Ellie couldn't have agreed with her sister more. 'And I suggest that the sooner you give him that choice, the better it will be for everyone,' she added caustically.

Daniel stared at the two of them, an admiring look in his eyes now. 'Couple of tough cookies, aren't you?' he finally drawled, standing up.

Tough? She and Beth? He had to be joking! Oh, they had had a hard time of it after their parents had had to leave the running of the hotel to them two years ago, and it hadn't been all that easy for them to keep things going. But tough? Was that why Beth was literally wasting away, wondering if her marriage was going to end in divorce? Was that why she herself had trouble sleeping at nights, worrying about the possibility of losing the hotel? Tough? No, she somehow didn't think so.

'If that's what you choose to think, Mr Thackery,' she told him coolly. 'Peter has gone off duty for a few hours,' she continued briskly, 'but he should be back at about four to prepare for dinner. Or you could call him at home and arrange to meet him before then. I think I have his home telephone number here.' She turned to the book on her desk.

'I thought you might have,' Daniel returned drily. 'Don't bother, Ellie.' He shook his head. 'I can see him later this afternoon when he comes back on duty.'

'Well, if there's nothing else?' she said pointedly as he made no effort to leave, determinedly ignoring the jibe he had made about Peter's home telephone number.

'Oh, but there is.' He strolled over to the door, his hand poised on the handle. 'I also want to thank you, Ellie.'

She blinked, feeling the heated colour entering her cheeks, shooting Beth an uncomfortable glance. What on earth did he have to thank her for? If it was anything to do with last night—!

She swallowed hard. 'For what?'

He met her gaze mockingly, laughing blue eyes looking straight into wary green. 'For not wearing Sapphire today,' he finally drawled. 'Your thoughtfulness is much appreciated.'

Her choice of perfume today had nothing to do with being thoughtful towards Daniel; she simply hadn't thought about it at all. And for Daniel to give Beth the impression that it was otherwise would only add to her sister's speculation about the two of them. In fact, she could already see her sister eyeing the two of them with renewed interest!

'Your appreciation is misplaced, Daniel,' Ellie bit out tautly. 'I—'

'No, don't spoil it, Ellie,' he cut in with husky softness. 'Leave me some illusions in life,' was his parting comment as, with a mocking grin, he left the office.

Ellie was speechless for several long seconds, gazing dumbstruck at the door Daniel had closed so quietly behind him. It was turning to see Beth watching her with some amusement that finally broke the moment.

'That man has no illusions,' she snapped disgustedly. 'And he makes no effort to create any either!'

'Is that not a good thing?' Beth frowned. 'At least you know up front with him exactly what you're getting—that he's exactly what he appears to be,' she added with some bitterness.

As Beth had learned that James wasn't... 'Beth, don't you think you should make a bit more of an effort to try and find out where James is?' she suggested gently, persisting even though she saw the way her sister stiffened defensively. 'Just sitting here waiting to hear from him isn't achieving anything.'

Beth stood up and walked over to the door, her face pale. 'I will contact him. When I have to,' she added shakily.

Ellie frowned. 'What do you mean by that?'

Her sister's gaze was evasive. 'Nothing.'

'Beth—'

'Let's just leave it, Ellie,' she said tautly. 'I have some work I need to do,' she muttered, before hurrying from the room.

Ellie sat down behind the desk, making no effort to start on her own work. She didn't know what she was going to do about Beth, especially now that her sister had even stopped talking to her about her problem, but something would have to change. And soon—because Beth was emotionally near to breaking point.

'Hi.' Peter looked into the office after knocking briefly on the door. 'Do you have a few minutes?'

Ellie had looked up with some gratitude at the sound of the knock on the door; she had been working on bills and invoices for most of the day, and had had no idea it was this late. Four-thirty—obviously Daniel had spoken to Peter.

'Of course,' she assured him invitingly. 'Come in. Did you have a pleasant few hours off?' She smiled across the width of the desk at him.

'Fine.' He nodded dismissively, sitting in the chair opposite hers. 'I've come back to strike while the iron is hot.' He grinned at her.

Ellie frowned her puzzlement. 'Sorry?'

'I hope that isn't another refusal,' he teased lightly. 'I've been thinking all day of places where we might go.'

He had lost her somewhere. As soon as she had realised who her visitor was she had begun to prepare herself for the fact that he was here to hand in his resignation.

'When?' She frowned, desperately trying to attune herself to the conversation.

'Well, Monday is my next evening off, so—'

'You're talking about the two of us going out for the evening!' she realised suddenly.

'Of course.' He shook his head mockingly. 'You haven't forgotten your acceptance this morning already?'

No, she hadn't forgotten it—she just hadn't thought it would be on the list of priorities in Peter's mind just now. Perhaps Daniel hadn't had a chance to speak to him yet . . .

'No, of course not.' She frowned again. 'What did you have in mind?' She could organise with Beth for her own evening off to be on Monday too.

'Well, you could look a little happier about it, for a start,' he laughed teasingly.

'Sorry.' She gave a rueful smile. 'I just— Monday evening would be lovely. And I'll leave the choice of where we go to you.'

'I'll look forward to it.' Peter stood up. 'Now I had better go, before the kitchen staff massacre the vegetables!'

Ellie chuckled. 'I must admit there's been a vast improvement in presentation since you took over.'

He grinned as he opened the door. 'Just as well I'm staying, then, isn't it?'

She blinked, frowning.

'I turned down Daniel Thackery's offer, Ellie,' Peter told her mockingly before leaving.

He *had* spoken to Daniel!

And, apparently, had turned down the other man's offer.

What did Daniel think of that...?

CHAPTER SIX

'You did a good job on Osborne,' Daniel bit out harshly.

Ellie faced him across the width of her private lounge. Her heart had started to thump more frequently than usual as soon as Daniel had knocked on the door a few seconds ago. She had known it had to be him—had been expecting this meeting ever since Peter had made his announcement earlier.

She faced him coolly. 'I beg your pardon?'

'Osborne,' he rasped, striding forcefully into the room. 'What sort of inducements did you use to get him to stay on here?' he added scathingly. 'You can't afford to pay him any more. Or to hire him an assistant. So what did you use?' Daniel looked at her with steely eyes.

Ellie stood her ground, not showing by so much as one nervous movement that this furiously angry Daniel disturbed her. Because he did. Always in the past he had been either mocking or derisive, and perfectly controlled, but at this moment in time he looked more than a little angry. And it was now a good three hours since he had spoken to Peter, so God knew what his mood had been like immediately after that. Perhaps she should feel grateful that he had waited.

She wished now that she hadn't changed when she'd come through from the office—she was wearing fitted denims and a short blue jumper, with her hair loose about her shoulders and her feet bare of shoes. Well, she hadn't thought she was going to see any guests for the next couple of hours, and had felt like being comfortable in her own home. And this *was* her home, and she was off duty—and this conversation was surely business? She didn't have to put up with this abuse!

She glanced at her wristwatch. 'I should be back on duty in two hours, Daniel. Perhaps we can have this conversation then?' she suggested distantly.

His mouth tightened. 'What's wrong with now?'

'I'm off duty—'

'And does that mean your brain ceases to function?' he scorned. 'That you can't involve yourself in conversation on a level higher than—?'

'There's no need to be insulting!' Ellie cut in coldly.

'Isn't there?' he taunted harshly. 'You got to Osborne when I had specifically asked you not to do so. You—'

'I didn't mention your proposition to Peter!' she interrupted protestingly.

'Forgive me if I don't believe you—'

'I don't give a damn whether you believe me or not,' she told him heatedly. 'And I don't "forgive" you for calling me a liar either.' Her eyes flashed deeply green. 'Exactly what reasons did Peter give you for turning down your offer?' She was interested in those herself . . .

'Personal ones. It doesn't take a genius to work out that you figure somewhere amongst those reasons!' Daniel accused her scathingly.

Ellie's top lip curled scornfully. 'It takes a mind like yours to work out something like that,' she said with obvious disgust. 'I had absolutely nothing to do with Peter turning down your offer.' Accepting one dinner invitation from the man did not count.

Daniel's eyes were narrowed in calculation as he continued to look at her. 'What is it with you, Ellie?' he finally asked slowly, his tone just cold now, that fierce anger of a few moments ago seeming to have faded. 'You hang onto those people around you like grim death,' he explained at her puzzled look. 'Are you frightened of being left alone? Is that it?'

'I don't know what you're talking about,' she dismissed impatiently. 'I've already told you—I didn't talk to Peter and I had nothing to do with his decision to turn your offer down.'

'We aren't just talking about Osborne.' Daniel shook his head, still looking at her thoughtfully. 'I don't understand you at all—'

'No one is asking you to!' Ellie returned irritably.

'But I think I want to.' He spoke softly, his expression thoughtful. 'You're a beautiful woman—'

'Thank you so much!' she said with sarcasm.

'Young, beautiful, with a spirited nature that most men would be tempted to try and harness—to tame it would be to take away that fieriness about you that is so intriguing—'

'Daniel, I'm really not interested in your opinion of me!' she cut in agitatedly, embarrassed at having someone—especially Daniel—describe her in those terms. For one thing she had never thought of herself

as beautiful, and for another she didn't want to hear
that Daniel was intrigued by her fieriness!

'I'm aware of that!' he bit out grimly. 'But you're
going to hear it anyway!'

'I—'

'Stop saying what you do and don't want and listen
to someone else for a change!' he insisted harshly.
'For God's sake, woman, I realise this hotel is important to you, but there's a big world out there just
waiting for you to take an interest in it. The world
doesn't start and end with this hotel, you know. At
least,' he continued firmly as she would have interrupted again, 'it shouldn't. Don't you want all the
normal things a woman of your age wants? Don't you
want a home of your own? A family?'

'Of course I do,' she returned heatedly, feeling very
much under attack. 'But it isn't as easy as that—'

'Why isn't it?' he demanded to know.

'I have responsibilities, people who rely on me.' She
shook her head, her cheeks red with agitation. What
business was it of his how she lived her life anyway?
'What I want for my own life comes way down on
the list of priorities.'

Daniel gave an impatient sigh. 'Why does it?
Haven't you realised yet that if you're happy then the
people around you tend to be the same way?'

'I am happy,' she told him defensively.

'Since when?' Daniel scorned.

Her face became flushed with anger. She wasn't
unhappy; she just wasn't particularly happy either.
But that was none of his business. None at all. 'You
have no right—'

'Of course I have the right.' Daniel moved deter-minedly towards her. 'I've held you in my arms, Ellie.' He stood directly in front of her now, only inches away but not quite touching. 'I've kissed you, felt you respond to me. I know the passionate warmth you're capable of. I'd hate all that to go to waste and for you to become a dried-up old prune of a spinster!'

Ellie glared up at him. '"Bitter and twisted"?'

'Exactly!' He grinned in the face of her fierce expression.

It was probably that grin that annoyed her more than his actual words, and for a moment she allowed her anger full rein, her arm swinging up in an arc.

'I don't think so, Ellie,' Daniel drawled as he easily reached out and grasped her arm, his fingers tight but not painful. 'All that fire going to waste,' he mur-mured regretfully, the darkness of his gaze roving ca-ressingly over her flushed face.

'It isn't—'

'Ellie, stop fighting everything and everyone,' he advised softly, his other hand moving up to lightly cup one side of her face, his thumb caressing against her lips as he gently parted them before his head lowered and his mouth claimed hers.

This was getting to be too much of a habit with this man. He couldn't just walk in here, verbally attack her and then proceed to kiss her until she couldn't think straight!

And that was exactly what was happening! Her in-itial resistance quickly turned into a melting sensation in her body, her arms curving up about his neck as she returned the kiss, her lips tingling with sensation as Daniel lightly ran his tongue over them, fiery heat warming her now.

Being in Daniel Thackery's arms, being kissed by him, was like nothing she had ever known before, and she gasped her pleasure as one of his hands caressed her back beneath the short jumper, his hand warm against her flesh, fingers lightly touching. Her gasp became a groan as that hand moved to lightly cup her breast through the silky material of her bra, fingertips brushing against the hardened nipple.

His lips were against her arched throat now, his breath hot, his tongue moist and searching, and pleasure was coursing through her as he probed the hollows at the base of her neck. And all the time his hands caressed and cupped her breast, his thumbtip moving rhythmically against her nipple now, evoking a need inside Ellie that cried out to be assuaged.

She offered no resistance as he released the catch on her bra, and her fingers entangled in the dark thickness of his hair as he raised her jumper and lowered his head to the creamy softness of her bared breasts, cradling him to her as moist lips closed possessively over one taut, inviting nipple, suckling, drawing the turgid pinkness into the waiting warmth of his mouth.

Heat fired her body, a restless heat that cried out for something more, bringing a deeper need that made her want to be even closer to him, to be part of him.

She clung to him as he swung her up into his arms and carried her over to the sofa, her face buried in his neck as he lowered her down into its softness. Her eyes were dark with pleading as he paused briefly to look questioningly down at her, and her breath caught in her throat as he answered that pleading by lowering the lean length of his body down onto hers.

Ellie gazed at him in wonder as he claimed that hardened nipple once again, watching as he licked and caressed with the moistness of his tongue, feeling his thighs now moving against hers with rhythmic pleasure.

He was hard against her, answering some of her need. But not all of it. Not all of it! She still wanted more . . .

Daniel pulled her jumper up over her head, dispensing with her bra completely too, looking down at her bared breasts with darkened eyes and cupping them before slowly lowering his head and kissing each rosy tip in turn, paying homage to their beauty.

'You're a very beautiful woman, Ellie,' he told her huskily, looking up.

She had never thought of herself as such, had the usual insecurities that most people suffered concerning the attractiveness of their body, and had always considered parts of her too small and other parts of her too big. But if Daniel thought she was beautiful then at that moment she felt that she truly was.

She gave a soft, throaty laugh, drawing him down to her, silently inviting him to kiss her once again. His mouth claimed hers, his tongue no longer caressing her lips but moving searchingly into her mouth, and his thighs pressed against hers, telling her of his own arousal.

When his hand moved to the button of her denims she gave a low groan, and as the zip slowly slid downwards the heat in her body increased. When she felt the warmth of his hand against her through her silky panties she thought she was going to lose control totally.

Daniel raised his head to look down at her passion-flushed face. 'Now, isn't it more fun when you stop fighting?' he murmured huskily.

Ellie blinked up at him, cold reality taking over. She was lying here, on the sofa, semi-naked, with Daniel Thackery. Daniel Thackery!

What was she doing? How could she possibly have responded to this man—a man who had been nothing but insulting and condescending ever since the first moment she'd met him? She had to be suffering from temporary insanity, had to be out of her—

'Ellie?' He shook his head as he saw the horrified panic in her face. 'Ellie, no—'

She pushed him away from her, unable to look at him as she struggled to her feet to snatch up her jumper and pull it down over her head. Without her bra, and with her breasts still aroused, the jumper wasn't really much protection against her nakedness—but it was better than nothing!

'You have to go, Daniel,' she told him woodenly, still unable to let her gaze meet his, staring somewhere over his shoulder.

He made no effort to stand up. 'Why do I?' he returned softly.

Her eyes flashed deeply green. 'Don't be ridiculous, Daniel,' she snapped scornfully. 'This should never have happened—'

'"This"?' Daniel sat back on the sofa, watching her with narrowed eyes. 'We're two adults, Ellie, who are obviously attracted to each other—'

'We are *not* attracted to each other!' Ellie burst in, two bright spots of colour in her cheeks.

'Don't be even more ridiculous, Ellie,' Daniel dismissed scathingly. 'If we were any more attracted to each other we would have gone up in flames together a few minutes ago!'

Oh, God! Ellie closed her eyes. The humiliation of it. How was she going to get through the rest of this man's stay at the hotel after what had just happened between them? Because she didn't think, after Peter's refusal of his offer, that Daniel would be leaving just yet; he didn't seem to be the sort of man who gave up at the first refusal.

'Ridiculous or not,' she bit out tautly, 'I want you to go.'

Daniel looked at her wordlessly for several long seconds, and then he stood up slowly. 'I will leave, Ellie—but only because I can see you're agitated. Our conversation is far from over,' he added grimly.

Conversation? The only conversation they had been having had been on a purely physical level. And how close *that* had come to reaching its conclusion! And 'agitated' didn't even begin to describe how she felt at the moment. 'Devastated' better described it!

'I happen to think it is.' She turned away, her arms wrapped protectively about herself. Why didn't he just go? Before she crumpled into a heap...

'Ellie—'

'Just go!' Her control was in danger of cracking completely.

He slowly crossed the room to stand just in front of her. 'You're a woman of twenty-seven, Ellie,' he murmured softly, shaking his head slightly. 'What happened between us just now wasn't so terrible. Or so tragic,' he added ruefully.

Maybe not for him. Of course not for him! This man was getting married next week—and yet he felt no guilt over what had just happened between them. And she shouldn't continue to let him see that it had upset her, either; that would be showing her own inexperience. And she had no intention of giving him that satisfaction.

'I didn't say it was,' she bit out, her eyes flashing rebelliously. 'It was more like a mistake.'

He frowned darkly. 'I don't consider it that either. Unless... Are you frightened of what Osborne's reaction might be if he should get to hear about it?' Daniel scorned. 'Do you think perhaps he might review your relationship if he were to know about us?'

Ellie stared at him. Was that the reason he—? 'Even if he did, he certainly wouldn't come to work for you either, would he?' Ellie challenged contemptuously.

Daniel's eyes narrowed to icy slits. 'Is that why you did it?' he said coldly. 'So you could tell Osborne I tried to seduce you?' He shook his head disgustedly. 'You have a problem, Ellie. A severe problem,' he

added gratingly, turning away from her dismissively.
'I feel sorry for you. And for anyone who gets involved with you.'

She glared at him. 'You know nothing about me,
Daniel. Absolutely nothing.'

He stood beside the door now. 'I know enough,'
he said flatly. 'It seems a pity, because I quite— Never
mind.' He shook his head self-derisively. 'Do your
worst where Osborne is concerned; it's his future
you're deliberately narrowing—for your own ends!'
The door closed behind him with a forceful slam.

Do her worst where Peter was concerned? Daniel
couldn't really think she would want anyone else to
know of her humiliation just now? Because she most
certainly didn't! Far from wanting anyone else to
know, she wanted to block the whole incident from
her own mind. Although she had a feeling that was
going to be impossible to do...

'You look a little pale, Ellie.' Beth looked at her, concerned, as Ellie took over from her on Reception a
couple of hours later. 'Are you feeling all right?'

Far from it! Once Daniel had left she had gathered
her scattered wits together—and her scattered
clothes!—and gone to have a long soak in the bath,
sure that the bath would help soothe her. But once
she had undressed and seen the faint redness on her
breasts, from Daniel's slightly abrasive chin, she had
felt far from soothed. Someone else looking at her
nakedness probably wouldn't have noticed that slight
redness against her otherwise creamy skin, but Ellie
was all too aware of those marks.

And she still was—felt as if her earlier intimacy with Daniel was written all over her face for all to see.

'Fine.' She avoided Beth's searching gaze, shuffling needlessly through some papers on the desk-top.

'You don't look it,' her sister persisted, still frowning. 'I don't mind staying on here for another few hours, Ellie, if you aren't—'

'I said I'm all right!' she bit out through gritted teeth, instantly feeling contrite as Beth looked hurt by her vehemence. 'Sorry, Beth .' She touched her sister's arm apologetically. 'I didn't mean to shout at you. But I really am feeling fine—more than capable of taking over here.' Besides, being on Reception would keep her busy, stop her thinking too much about what had happened earlier with Daniel. Left alone in the privacy of their living quarters, she would have far too much time to brood.

'Well . . . if you're sure.' Beth looked far from convinced. 'I—er—I was talking to Daniel earlier,' she began tentatively.

Ellie felt the colour drain from her cheeks. Surely Daniel hadn't talked to her own sister about what had happened between them? How could he—?

'He said he hasn't seen James since he left here,' Beth continued frowningly.

James? But—

'You told me to forget all about the subterfuge and just ask.' Her sister grimaced. 'So I did. Daniel says he hasn't seen James for several months.'

Now she realised what her sister meant. But if Daniel hadn't seen James how had he known about Peter? Daniel might have told Beth he hadn't seen her husband recently, but Ellie wasn't sure she believed

him. Although she had no intention of asking him
about it herself.

'And he doesn't know where he is either?' Ellie
pressed.

Beth looked perplexed. 'I must admit that wasn't
what I asked him...'

'Then perhaps you should have done,' she returned
drily. One thing she had learnt about Daniel was that
he was an extremely clever man. If Beth hadn't
specifically asked if he knew of James's whereabouts,
then Daniel wouldn't specifically have said whether
he knew or not either!

Her sister grimaced again. 'I doubt there's time
now; Daniel booked a table for breakfast at seven-
thirty in the morning.'

Ellie shrugged. 'Then talk to him later—'

'But I can't. Oh, dear, I forgot to tell you that bit.'
Beth frowned. 'Daniel is leaving straight after
breakfast.'

He was leaving! It was all rather sudden, wasn't
it...? Of course, Peter had turned down his offer,
but somehow she hadn't thought of Daniel as a man
who would give up at the first obstacle in the way of
something he wanted as badly as he seemed to want
Peter to work for him. He hadn't with her!

Not that she thought for a moment that what had
happened—almost happened!—between them had
anything to do with Daniel leaving. She very much
doubted that Daniel ever let what was happening in
his private life interfere with his business intentions.
No, Daniel had an altogether different reason for his
sudden departure tomorrow. And maybe it wasn't so

sudden; he was supposed to be marrying in a matter of days...

'I see,' she answered Beth tightly. 'In that case, I'll sort his bill out before I go off duty.'

Her sister nodded distractedly. 'But what do I do about James?' she wailed.

Ellie frowned across at her. 'What do you want to do?'

Tears misted Beth's eyes. 'I don't know! I do know I can't go on like this, not knowing exactly what's happening. Why doesn't he contact me, Ellie? Do something?'

'Why don't you?' she reasoned gently.

'James knows where I am; I haven't a clue where he is!' her sister protested.

'You could always telephone his parents,' Ellie suggested.

Beth shook her head. 'I don't know if they know about us—the separation, I mean. And if they don't I don't want to be the one to tell them. Daniel was my only hope.' She sighed heavily.

But if Beth hadn't asked Daniel the right questions in the right way then she wouldn't have got straightforward answers from him, Ellie was sure of it.

'You wouldn't try having one last talk with him for me, would you?' Beth looked at her appealingly.

'Me?' Ellie looked startled. 'Oh, no, Beth, I couldn't. I really could—'

'Ellie, I'm pregnant,' Beth burst in, her face pale. 'And don't immediately tell me I have to find James and tell him that; I don't want him back under those circumstances,' she said agitatedly.

Beth must have known that that was exactly what she had been about to tell her; James had a right to know that he was going to be a father. But at the same time, even as her sister spoke so vehemently, Ellie knew that she wouldn't want any man to come back into her life either just because she was expecting his child. It would have to be because he wanted to come back to her, and for no other reason. God, what a mess!

And this baby was what Beth had wanted for so long. How sad that it should have happened now, when the couple had separated.

'You see, I thought if I could just talk to James . . . Oh, not about the baby.' Beth shook her head firmly. 'If we get back together it won't be for that reason only. But we can't even begin to talk when he won't contact me and I don't know where he is. And once the baby begins to show . . .' She gave a decisive shake of her head.

Beth, Ellie knew, wouldn't talk to James about anything then—her pride wouldn't let her. Ellie could understand that, but at the same time . . .

'Will you speak to Daniel before he leaves?' Beth looked at her pleadingly once more. 'If you could just find out where James is, I could attempt to sort it out from there.'

What a dilemma! But it was one, Ellie knew, in which her own pride would have to take second place; Beth's wellbeing, and that of her baby, had to take priority. Which meant that Ellie would have to talk to Daniel in the morning before he left . . .

CHAPTER SEVEN

DESPITE all her best efforts, Ellie knew that she was pale the next morning as she waited at the reception desk. She had seen Daniel go into breakfast, knew it was only a matter of time before he came out of the dining room to pay his bill.

She wasn't really supposed to be on reception duty this morning, but it had taken very little effort to re-organise it so that she was. But it wasn't effort that was needed this morning, it was confidence—the confidence to talk to Daniel just as if that scene between them yesterday evening had never taken place. For Beth's sake she had to be able to do that...

It hadn't been an easy night for her, plagued as she had been by memories of her time in Daniel's arms. She had never responded to any man in the way she had with Daniel. And she had tried to understand why it should be him she responded to. To no avail. He was everything she disliked in a man—too rich, too powerful, too attractive, too—everything! Not only that, he was going to marry someone else next week!

Then what had she been doing the night before?

She hadn't been 'doing' anything; the whole thing had been beyond her control, beyond—

'Good morning, Ellie,' greeted his harshly derisive voice. 'Could I have my bill, please?'

She had been so lost in the torment of her thoughts that she hadn't even noticed Daniel's approach to the desk, and she felt herself turn even paler as she looked up at him. He was wearing a business suit, and she could only assume he was leaving here to continue his working day.

'The bill, Ellie,' he prompted softly as he received no response to his initial request, looking across at her with narrowed eyes. 'How are you today?'

Not feeling quite herself, that was for sure! Her usual fire and fight seemed to have temporarily deserted her. At least, she hoped it was temporary! She was just so numbed by her own behaviour, and response, that she didn't know herself any more. And it was all because of this man!

'That's better,' Daniel drawled derisively as he saw the angry flash in those deeply emerald eyes, leaning his elbows on the high desk. 'A forlorn-looking Ellie is not something I'm familiar with,' he added mockingly.

A forlorn-looking Ellie was not something *she* was familiar with either!

'Do you have time to come through to the private office for a few minutes before you leave?' she requested hardily.

He raised dark brows. 'Why?'

He wasn't about to be in the least helpful about this, she could see! 'Obviously I need to talk to you in private,' she bit out tautly.

Daniel gave her a searching glance for long, seemingly timeless seconds, and then he gave a slow nod of his head. 'I can spare a few minutes,' he agreed after a brief glance at his wristwatch.

Everything about this man put her teeth on edge; how gracious of him to be able to spare her 'a few minutes' of his precious time! She— But this was no good; she was doing this for Beth; her own personal feelings towards Daniel would have to be put firmly in the background if they were to have any conversation at all.

She led the way through to the private office, very aware of Daniel behind her, of his gaze on the length of her body. This was so much harder than she had imagined—and it had seemed nightmarish even in her imaginings!

'Yes?' he prompted in a businesslike tone once she had moved to stand determinedly behind the desk.

Irritation flashed in her eyes once again; this man gave no quarter, did he? 'I believe Beth spoke to you last night,' she began tentatively.

Daniel's expression was suddenly wary. 'Yes.'

Not very forthcoming, Ellie acknowledged—either his answer or his attitude. 'She asked you about James,' she reminded him a little impatiently.

'So she did,' he acknowledged noncommittally.

Ellie sighed; she didn't want to be having this conversation with him at all, was only doing it for her sister, and in the circumstances Daniel's lack of cooperation was the last thing she felt like dealing with. But then when had he behaved any differently?

'And you said you haven't seen James for several months.' She continued to watch him closely, trying

to gauge his reaction to the conversation—and, Daniel
being Daniel, there wasn't one!

He had to be the most enigmatic man she had ever
met! Except when they were in each other's arms, she
slowly acknowledged. Then he made no effort to hide
his desire for her. Oh, God, she was at it again—
wandering off into fantasyland; she had to forget that
Daniel and she had ever been in each other's arms.
It had been madness, pure and simple.

He gave a brief nod of his head. 'That's right, I
haven't,' he bit out dismissively.

Ellie gave an inclination of her head, having already
known what his answer was going to be. 'Then let me
put it another way—have you *spoken* to James
recently?'

Daniel looked at her consideringly, a slow smile
breaking the harshness of his expression, his body relaxing its defensive attitude somewhat. 'Shall we sit
down, Ellie?' he suggested smoothly. 'I think this
conversation may take longer than either of us initially expected,' he added drily.

In other words, he *had* spoken to James! She had
been sure, when Beth had told her last night of her
conversation with this man, that unless the question
had been put in a specific way Daniel would have
found a way of evading the issue.

She had no idea what Daniel had thought this conversation was going to be about, although she could
take an educated guess. Well, he was wrong; she
wanted to forget what had happened between the two
of them, not talk about it—to anyone!

Ellie sat down abruptly behind the desk, waiting while Daniel lowered his lean length into the chair opposite before resuming the conversation. 'Have you spoken to James?' she prompted determinedly.

He looked across at her with narrowed blue eyes. 'And if I have? Why are you so interested, Ellie?'

She frowned. 'I am naturally concerned for Beth—'

'That must be a first!' Daniel bit out scathingly, his expression one of contempt.

She recoiled as if he had physically struck her, her face paling anew. What on earth did he mean? And on what did he base such a scathing assumption? Since her parents had moved abroad, leaving the two of them to run the hotel, she and Beth had become closer than ever before; what on earth had made Daniel think she wasn't concerned for her sister's happiness?

As far as she was aware, nothing had happened at the hotel since his arrival that could possibly have given him that impression; she and Beth had been their usual selves, their relationship running with its usual harmony. What did Daniel think he was doing, accusing her of being uncaring where Beth was concerned? She wouldn't be having this conversation with him at all if she didn't care so deeply about her sister, and her sister's happiness!

'You didn't like that remark, did you, Ellie?' Daniel drawled icily, watching her through narrowed lids. 'The truth hurts, does it?' he scorned.

Her eyes flashed deeply green. 'It might do—if it were the truth! But it isn't.' She shook her head. 'Of

course I'm concerned for Beth. And for the state her
marriage seems to have deteriorated into. She—'

'It doesn't *seem* to have done anything, Ellie,'
Daniel rasped harshly. 'Beth and James's relationship
is a damned mess—as you very well know!' he added
accusingly.

It was more of a mess than he could possibly realise—because he didn't know anything about the
baby.

She gave a deep sigh. 'With a little bit of help from
you— specifically, information as to where James can
be found—I'm trying to help sort that out,' she told
him impatiently.

'Interfering in other people's lives again, Ellie?'
Daniel scorned derisively. 'Aren't you ever going to
learn?' He shook his head disgustedly. 'Haven't you
done enough damage already?'

Ellie stared at him with wide, puzzled eyes, and then
she realised. 'If you're referring to Peter again,' she
said with a sigh, 'I can only reassure you—once
more—that I had absolutely nothing to do with his
refusal of your offer.'

Daniel's mouth twisted. 'I doubt that very much,'
he bit out disgustedly. 'But that wasn't the damage I
was referring to. You have to know what a bone of
contention you've been between Beth and James
during the last year.'

'*I* have?' she gasped disbelievingly. It was the first
she had heard of it; she and James had always got
along perfectly well together. Daniel had to be mistaken. Or else he was just trying to distract her from
what she was really trying to talk to him about—

namely James's whereabouts. Which she was more than ever convinced that he was aware of! 'I think you're mistaken there, Daniel—'

'Am I?' he scorned. 'One of us is mistaken about a lot of things—and it isn't me!'

She stood up abruptly. 'No, it wouldn't be, would it?' she accused him challengingly. 'The great Daniel Thackery can do no wrong, can he? At least in his own eyes!' She glared down at him.

Daniel looked up at her unwaveringly, not at all perturbed by her fiery response. 'I think you have that the wrong way round too, Ellie,' he replied with infuriating calm. '*You* seem to be the one—in *your* own eyes!—who can do no wrong. Especially where Beth is concerned.'

Ellie continued to look down at him, frowning darkly. 'I don't understand,' she finally said slowly, unnerved by his steady gaze.

Daniel sighed heavily. 'No,' he murmured softly. 'I don't believe you do.'

She was stung by his almost pitying tone. 'But I'm sure you're going to tell me!' Her eyes sparkled defiantly.

He continued to look at her for long, searching moments. 'Is it just me, Ellie? Or are you this prickly with everyone?'

'It's not a question of being "prickly", Daniel,' she returned waspishly. 'You have made an accusation, and I would like an explanation for that accusation.' She met his gaze in steady demand.

He shook his head slowly. 'I'm not so sure that you would,' he murmured softly, frowning slightly.

His slightly patronising tone annoyed her even more. 'Allow me to be the judge of what I do and don't want to know,' she bit out coldly, her gaze meeting his challengingly.

His mouth twisted. 'Maybe you *aren't* the best judge of that, Ellie,' he taunted. 'You seem to think the time you've spent in my arms has been a mistake—I happen to think otherwise!'

Heated colour flooded her cheeks at his reminder of times she would rather forget. But then she was sure that he knew exactly how she felt about that— was equally sure that he knew exactly what he was doing by mentioning the subject at all. He was obviously hoping to disconcert her totally, and distract her attention from her original question. Which wasn't going to happen!

'We were talking about Beth,' she reminded him pointedly.

Daniel shook his head. 'No—you were talking about Beth. I would much rather talk about you— and your response to me.' He raised mocking brows.

Her eyes flashed deeply green. 'I don't have a response—'

Daniel was on his feet and at her side before she really had time to take in what he was doing, and his sudden appearance in front of her surprised her into silence.

Ellie looked up at him with shocked eyes; for a big man he moved with surprising agility and stealth. And at the moment he looked furiously angry too.

'Oh, you have a response, Ellie,' he bit out harshly, his hand under her chin as he brought her face dangerously close to his. 'You're a passionate woman who, for some reason beyond my comprehension, takes a delight in running other people's lives and ignoring the needs of your own—'

'If you're implying that I need you—'

'You need someone like me, Ellie,' he insisted with cold determination. 'Otherwise one day you're going to wake up and find yourself an old woman, having had no life or family of your own!'

She shook her head. 'You don't know what you're talking about,' she dismissed scathingly.

'I know *you*, Ellie—no matter what you might think to the contrary. For a while there I even thought— Well, never mind what I thought. You would have to change a hell of a lot in the way you think of people and relationships for me to even consider getting involved with you again.'

'Again?' Ellie echoed in an outraged voice. 'We haven't been involved a first time, let alone a second!' She glared at him incredulously.

His mouth twisted in hard mockery. 'Oh, we've been involved, Ellie.' He nodded. 'What's the saying?' he mused softly, his hand relaxing its grip on her chin, his thumb gently caressing. 'We had an interesting relationship—I just wish you'd been there! I do wish that, Ellie,' he added quietly, his head bending slightly so that he could run his lips lightly over the top of hers. 'Lighten up on life, Ellie,' he advised her. 'Maybe then it will lighten up on you.'

And that was his parting comment! One moment he had been standing in front of her, tormenting the life out of her as usual, and the next he had gone—

disappearing from her life as suddenly as he had entered it.

'Lighten up on life. Maybe then it will lighten up on you.' What, exactly, had he meant by that? Of course she took life seriously—it was a serious business. But she wasn't altogether sure that that was what he'd meant...

And, she suddenly realised, by changing the subject in that altogether personal way, he had neatly avoided answering her questions about James. Damn him! She had been so determined she wouldn't be sidetracked, and yet somehow Daniel had managed to do it. He hadn't told her anything about James she didn't already know—namely that her brother-in-law was obviously reluctant to be found until he was ready.

And Daniel had also, Ellie acknowledged with a self-derisive groan, left the hotel without paying his bill!

She hadn't even managed to get *that* right where that man was concerned!

'Well, I may have managed to persuade you to join me for dinner at long last,' Peter said drily, 'but you don't seem to be enjoying yourself very much!'

Ellie gave a guilty start, looking across the width of the table at him. 'I'm sorry,' she groaned, realising that for the last five minutes she had been miles away, thinking of goodness knew what; Peter could have told her during that time that little green men from Mars had landed and she would probably have agreed with him!

Which wasn't very fair on him. As he'd said, this was the first time they had ever gone out together, and it had taken weeks of persuasion on his part; the least she owed him was to take an interest in his conversation.

But she had been distracted the last couple of days. Since Daniel had left... She freely—inwardly—acknowledged that. Outwardly there was no way she would ever have admitted that anything about Daniel Thackery had unsettled her normally ordered existence. But inside she was realising, more and more, that Daniel's statements had made her restless. And questioning. There were so many things she wanted answers to. And there was no way she could ask him!

'I really am sorry, Peter.' She reached across the table and gently touched his arm. 'I freely admit I was miles away then.' She gave a ruefully apologetic smile. 'What were you talking about?'

He laughed softly, his handsome face alight with humour. 'You do little or nothing for my ego, Ellie,' he said drily. 'But I do appreciate your honesty.'

'I'm sorry if I'm not being good company.' She shook her head. 'I have enjoyed my meal—honestly.'

The restaurant Peter had chosen for their evening out wasn't one she had been to before, being almost an hour's drive away from the hotel. But the food was very good, the service excellent, and her companion very attentive, and, as evenings went, Ellie knew she should have been having a marvellous time. But somehow she couldn't shake Daniel and that last conversation with him from her mind. He had seemed to be implying that Beth and James's marital problems had something to do with her...

Peter arched blond brows. 'But...?'

She laughed softly at his rueful expression. 'There is no "but".' She smiled. 'I've had a lovely time.'

Peter looked slightly disbelieving. 'Wherever you've been doesn't seem a very enjoyable place,' he said drily. 'You've been frowning most of the evening,' he explained at her puzzled expression.

'Oh, dear, have I?' Ellie grimaced.

He nodded. 'Are you still worried about Beth?'

'Oh, God, yes,' she confirmed heavily.

'She doesn't look too good, I must admit,' Peter sighed.

That had to be an understatement! Beth seemed to be suffering from morning sickness at the moment—except in her sister's case it seemed to go on all day! Poor Beth had been in bed most of today with the affliction, although strangely enough the nausea seemed to disappear completely in the evenings; her sister was turning into a night person—roaming around the hotel, raiding the refrigerator, and then spending the day in bed feeling totally sick. It was the baby, of course, and Ellie could only sympathise with her; she seemed to be of little other help as Beth preferred to be left alone.

What Beth really needed was her husband at her side. And Ellie was very aware of the fact that it was because she had once again lost her temper with Daniel that he had evaded telling her if he knew of James's whereabouts—which she was still utterly convinced that he did!

'She isn't feeling too good.' Ellie confirmed Peter's statement. 'But I just don't know what to do for the best.' She had thought about this so long and often that she had given herself a headache. And she was sure poor Peter didn't want to be bothered with her problems.

'Pride can be a terrible thing,' Peter said with a grimace.

'I'm not being proud.' She was stung into defending her behaviour towards Daniel. 'I was just—'

'I wasn't talking about you,' Peter cut in gently. 'I was talking about Beth and James.'

Oh, God; what an idiot she was. Damn Daniel—he clouded every other issue she tried to deal with.

'Sorry.' She gave a rueful smile. 'You talk as if you know from experience?' She looked at him curiously.

'I do.' He nodded, his expression grim. 'I thought I had it all at one time, Ellie—the thriving career, the good marriage, a baby daughter.' He shook his head. 'How wrong I was!'

Ellie hadn't realised Peter had been married, although for a man in his late thirties that wasn't perhaps unusual. Daniel wasn't married! The thought popped into her head unbidden. Damn Daniel—he might not be married yet, but he was soon going to be. Besides, he had no place in this conversation. 'What happened?' she softly prompted Peter.

He frowned. 'Well, as you may have noticed, in that list of assets to my life I mentioned my career first. I believed, mistakenly, that my wife should put it first too, that it was the axis around which the rest of our life revolved.' He shrugged. 'I put my career first, I admit that now, and when my wife had had enough of being second best she said goodbye and left.'

'But—'

'And I don't blame her, Ellie,' he continued firmly. 'That sort of arrogance has no place in a marriage— especially when there is a child involved. My wife was tired of sitting at home night after night, with only a small child for company, while I furthered my career—'

'But if it was for the two of you—'

'But was it?' Peter reasoned self-derisively. 'What did my wife get out of the relationship? A successful husband and a comfortable lifestyle? But it was a husband she never saw and a comfortable lifestyle that was empty when experienced on her own.

'I know, Ellie, because they were the arguments I used when Kate walked out, and those were her replies. Replies, I might add, that for months I refused to accept. Kate told me I would realise what she meant one day—and she was right. I *have* realised, Ellie; it's relationships that count, because if you don't have the right person at your side, then you don't really have anything!'

He spoke so vehemently that Ellie couldn't doubt that he meant it. And the history of his marriage answered so many of the questions she'd had concerning him. It also explained why he hadn't been interested in accepting Daniel's offer; Peter had already had all the success he could handle, and it had cost him his wife and daughter.

'Do you still see them?' Ellie prompted gently.

His mouth twisted. 'Why do you think I live in the area? Kate has remarried now, so there's no hope left there,' he acknowledged a little bleakly, 'but I still see Laura at the weekends. I've managed to retain quite a good relationship with my daughter and I would like it to remain that way.'

So now she had all the answers to her questions about Peter. But she was left with a few questions for herself. Pride was a dangerous thing, Peter had said, and in this case they weren't only dealing with Beth's pride where James was concerned but also Ellie's pride where Daniel was concerned; she was sure Daniel could help her with regard to the other couple—was still sure he knew where James was—but her pride was holding her back from asking him.

Was her pride costing Beth her marriage? Her chance at happiness? Because she was still convinced that Beth and James loved each other, and if someone didn't sort this mess out soon it was going to be too late. As it had been in Peter's case...

'Food for thought?' Peter looked at her curiously.

She pulled a face. 'Food for thought,' she acknowledged with a nod. 'I'm really sorry about your marriage, Peter.' It all sounded very sad.

'Don't be,' he dismissed quietly. 'Kate and I have managed to work out a sort of friendship, and I've maintained my relationship with Laura. I did quite well out of it—considering I had been such a selfish bastard for so long!'

There was still time for Beth and James, if someone would only give them a helping hand. And, Ellie realised, she was the only person who could do that. And the only way she could do it was by seeing Daniel once more...

CHAPTER EIGHT

'Well, well, well, I didn't realise your hotel was so desperate for money that you had to deliver unpaid bills personally!'

Ellie almost turned on her heel and walked away without even replying to the insulting taunt. She should have known Daniel wouldn't make this easy; when had he ever made anything easy for her?

It hadn't been easy getting away to see him at all—Beth had been very upset at her sudden departure. But the hotel was still in its quiet season, and Ellie had used the excuse of visiting an old schoolfriend. But as far as Beth was concerned, Ellie knew, her timing was awful. Beth needed her moral support now, if nothing else. And, if her sister did but know it, that was exactly what she was getting—because there was no way Ellie would have been at Daniel's apartment like this voluntarily.

He had opened the door to her himself seconds after her first ring, disconcerting Ellie before she'd even begun; she had expected him to have a housekeeper, to be asked to wait while Daniel was informed of her arrival. Instead he had suddenly been standing in front of her—his sarcasm not in the least diminished by the four days since they'd last met.

'I'm not here to talk about your bill,' she returned waspishly, her gaze meeting his defiantly.

129

'No?' He quirked mocking brows. 'Do we have anything else to talk about?'

Ellie drew in a deep, controlling breath. 'I hope so,' she replied steadily. 'You see, I—'

'Is this going to take long, Ellie?' Daniel gave an impatient glance at his watch. 'Only I have a business appointment in half an hour and I have to drive there.'

Ellie looked at her own watch. A business appointment at six-thirty at night? She had deliberately chosen to arrive at a time she'd believed he would be in from the office—late enough for him to be at home, but early enough that he wouldn't think she expected him to spend the evening with her. That was the last thing she wanted!

'I see.' She frowned. 'In that case, could I make an appointment to see you some time tomorrow?' She only intended staying in London a couple of days at the most—just long enough to see if Daniel would tell her where James was and then go and see her brother-in-law herself. But she very much doubted, if she were to ask Daniel now about James's whereabouts, that he would actually tell her. She needed time to talk to him about Beth and the baby; as far as she was concerned, telling Daniel wasn't telling James—it was only enlisting his help in a situation that was spiralling totally out of control.

'What's wrong with later this evening?' Daniel said distractedly. 'Look, come inside a minute, will you, Ellie? I'm not quite ready yet and my driver will be here any minute.'

Ellie followed him into what she was sure would be a luxurious apartment; it was unlikely that it would be anything else if it was owned by Daniel. But, unlike his hotel room during his stay, his home had a much more lived-in appearance—personal items cluttering the main living room, a dinner jacket thrown over one of the chairs. He now put on the jacket over his snowy white shirt and black trousers before moving to the mirror to straighten his tie.

Ellie frowned. 'But I thought you said you had a business appointment for the evening?' She looked confused.

His mouth twisted. 'Aperitifs do not take all evening,' he dismissed drily. 'Besides, I'll have concluded my business there within an hour and then I would like to have some dinner. You might as well join me.'

If wasn't the most gracious invitation she had ever received, but, remembering how strained their last parting had been, she thought it was probably the best one she was going to get from Daniel! Besides, what choice did she have?

He grinned at the emotions battling across her face. 'I think we had better have dinner together, Ellie, because I'm becoming more and more intrigued. Part of you seems to want to tell me to go to hell, and another part of you is making you swallow that down and accept my invitation. Accept it, Ellie,' he urged, grasping her shoulders lightly as he looked down encouragingly into her face. 'If nothing else, you'll have a good meal out of it.'

She looked up into his too handsome face—a face alight with mischief. His gaze was warm.

'Come on, Ellie,' he prompted impatiently. 'I don't have all night for you to make up your mind. I—' He broke off as the doorbell rang. 'That will be my driver.' He frowned. 'Well, Ellie, is it yes or no?'

'I—' She hesitated as the doorbell rang again.

Daniel glanced at the door with irritation. 'Could you get that for me? I just have to get my briefcase from the bedroom.' He left the room without waiting to see if she did as he asked, obviously taking it for granted that she would.

Which was typical, Ellie acknowledged as she went to open the door. Arrogance seemed to be Daniel's middle name. But she couldn't exactly blame him for that either; he was obviously a man used to giving orders and having them carried out.

Nevertheless, Ellie wasn't prepared to find 'Darling' standing on the doorstep! Daniel had said he had a business appointment, that his driver would be arriving any minute; he certainly hadn't given the impression that the beautiful blonde she'd seen him with at the hotel was going to be that driver!

'Hello.' The other woman smiled at her warmly, looking exotically beautiful in a sky-blue knee-length dress of pure silk. 'Is Daniel ready?'

Ellie just stared at her, not knowing quite what to say. Didn't 'Darling' think it was in the least odd that another woman had opened the door to Daniel's apartment? Ellie didn't think she would have been smiling in such a friendly way if the roles had been reversed!

'I believe so,' she finally answered gruffly. 'He—he's just gone to get his briefcase from—from the bedroom.' Heated colour darkened her cheeks as she said the last word. Which was ridiculous; she had never been anywhere near Daniel's bedroom!

'Fine.' The other woman nodded, her head tilted to one side as she looked at Ellie enquiringly. 'Don't I know you from somewhere?'

Ellie didn't think having possibly seen her about the hotel could be classed as knowing her. Besides, she didn't really want to get into a personal conversation with this woman; the less she had to do with Daniel's complicated personal life the better!

'I don't think so,' she dismissed easily. 'Won't you come in? I'm sure Daniel won't be long.' At least, she hoped he wouldn't. How long could it take to pick up a briefcase, for goodness' sake? She certainly didn't want to be left alone with 'Darling' for too long—had nothing whatsoever to talk to her about. The only thing they had in common was Daniel, and she certainly didn't want to talk about him!

'I'm Joanne, by the way.' The other woman held out her hand politely once they were in the main living room.

'Ellie,' she supplied abruptly, shooting anxious glances towards the bedroom Daniel had disappeared into minutes ago.

'Short for?' Joanne prompted lightly, elegantly lowering her diminutive figure into one of the armchairs.

Ellie frowned; not many people asked her that any more. She had no idea what her mother had been thinking of when she'd named her, but whatever it was she certainly hadn't envisaged her tall, red-haired daughter when she'd originally chosen the name.

'Giselle,' she muttered reluctantly.

The other woman smiled up at her. 'What a pretty name.'

But hardly suitable for someone of Ellie's stature and colouring, which was why it had very quickly been shortened to Ellie once she was through babyhood.

'What is?'

She inwardly cringed as Daniel came back into the room, looking at the two women curiously. No doubt he would have something sarcastic to say about the inappropriateness of her given name!

Joanne stood up in one smoothly elegant movement, her blonde hair swinging loose about her shoulders. 'Giselle, darling,' she explained warmly. 'It's a beautiful name.'

Ellie—Giselle—looked at him challengingly, daring him to say anything sarcastic about her name. For, being Daniel, he would have realised it was her name they were discussing.

'Beautiful,' he finally murmured, that light of mischief still in his eyes as he deliberately held her gaze for longer than was necessary.

Ellie met his look defiantly, daring him to say more—and knowing that he was more than capable of doing so! But she could see, after his brows had been raised briefly in her direction before he turned his attention back to Joanne, that he had decided not to do so in front of their audience. Ellie, however, didn't doubt that she hadn't heard the last on the subject; Daniel would enjoy teasing her.

'You may as well stay on here and wait for me,' he suggested practically. 'I shouldn't be long and it will save time afterwards.'

Stay on here, in his apartment? Didn't he mind leaving a relative stranger in his home? Apparently not. His expression was one of impatience as he waited for her answer. Ellie had to admit that she found the idea of being here while Daniel was out very strange indeed. And what if someone should telephone while he was out, or, even worse, actually come to visit? What was she—?

'I don't have time to argue with you, Ellie,' Daniel told her irritably, her answer obviously too long in coming for his liking. 'I really do have to go. We'll decide what we're going to do when I get back,' he informed her with his usual arrogance, preparing to leave.

'Nice to have met you, Ellie,' Joanne said with continuing warmth.

Ellie wasn't so sure that in the same circumstances she would have been as magnanimous as the other woman. 'And you,' she muttered uncomfortably.

'Perhaps I'll see you again,' Joanne continued as Daniel sorted distractedly through some papers in his open briefcase.

She doubted it! 'Maybe,' Ellie mumbled, wishing the two of them would just leave.

'Perhaps at the wedding on Saturday?'

The other woman was only making conversation to cover Daniel's distraction, Ellie knew, but she couldn't help staring at her when she heard this last question. Joanne was going to be present at Daniel's wedding to Angela on Saturday? This man didn't just have a complicated personal life; it was a veritable maze of mystery and intrigue! Thank God she wasn't a part of it!

'I don't think so,' she answered with dismissive finality.

'Are you ready, Joanne?' Daniel had seemed unaware of their conversation while he had been so preoccupied, and was now snapping shut his briefcase.

'Of course,' she assured him compliantly.

'You'll find all the usual coffee-making things in the kitchen.' Daniel turned briefly back to Ellie. 'Or if you want something stronger there's a bar over there.' He pointed uninterestedly towards a drinks cabinet. 'I'll only be an hour or so.'

Ellie felt like telling him that she was perfectly capable of entertaining herself for 'an hour or so' if necessary—but he wasn't there to tell, having already left the apartment with the lovely Joanne.

Ellie looked around her uncomfortably. She didn't much like the idea of staying here when Daniel wasn't actually at home; it was far too intimate a situation. But, by the same token, if he didn't mind, why should she? As long as his fiancée didn't ring or come here! Angela had sounded extremely waspish that day on the telephone, and Ellie didn't relish the idea of coming face to face with the other woman. Especially in Daniel's apartment!

But she couldn't just sit here either, afraid to move, and the idea of coffee sounded good. Besides, making it would pass some of the waiting time; she had built herself up to this meeting with Daniel and it was a bit of an anticlimax to have their conversation delayed this way.

The coffee was good, but after enjoying two cups she knew she had better stop; too much coffee and her nerves were going to be completely jumpy, and she was apprehensive enough already.

The telephone didn't ring at all, but her worst fears were realised about half an hour after Daniel's departure, when the shrill ringing of the doorbell heralded the arrival of a visitor. Could it be Angela, as she had dreaded? Surely Daniel couldn't have been stupid enough to go out with Joanne and have his fiancée due to arrive later in the evening? Daniel wasn't stupid at all, she knew that, so hopefully not. But he was arrogant... No, even *he* wasn't that arrogant, especially as there already appeared to be some sort of friction between the two women.

The doorbell rang a second time while these panicky thoughts were rushing through Ellie's mind, and it was with a sense of trepidation that she went to open the door.

The person she found standing on the other side of that door was positively the last person she had expected to see. Although it did answer that vital question for her...

'Ellie...!' James gasped, too astounded himself to hide his amazement at finding her there.

Well, at least now she knew that Daniel *had* spoken to her brother-in-law since he'd left Beth. She was too surprised at his presence here to be able to think of much else.

But if her sister looked pale and wan then James was faring little better; her brother-in-law had lost weight himself over the last month or so, his face thin and gaunt, lines beside his eyes and mouth. He looked as ill as Beth and was obviously just as unhappy. Which made the situation the two of them had found themselves in all the more ridiculous.

'You had better come in, James.' Ellie held the door open for him to enter.

He made no effort to move. 'I wanted to talk to Daniel,' he bit out stiltedly.

'I'm aware of that,' she acknowledged gently. 'He isn't here at the moment, but he should be back soon.' She looked at her wristwatch. 'Daniel said he would only be about an hour, and it's been almost that now. Do come in, James,' she invited again.

'I—'

'Beth misses you, James,' she put in softly as she sensed that he was about to refuse her invitation.

If anything he seemed to go paler, almost grey, as if the mention of his wife was almost too much for him. God, this was stupid; James was obviously missing Beth as much as she was missing him!

'Come in and I'll make you a cup of coffee—or something stronger,' Ellie encouraged. 'Talking to me isn't going to hurt you, James,' she added as he still made no move to enter the apartment.

'Of course it isn't, Ellie,' he acknowledged impatiently. 'I just—'

'Wouldn't you like to hear more about Beth?' she cut in temptingly.

'You never did play fair, Ellie,' James groaned, walking past her into the apartment, his jaw clenched as he fought to control his emotions.

'I'm not playing at all, James,' Ellie told him quietly as she watched him pour a glass of whisky for himself. He was perfectly at home with the layout of Daniel's apartment, indicating a familiarity of long standing. Damn Daniel! He could have saved Beth a lot of pain if he had just told them the truth last week! 'I very rarely do, James. You should know that,' she added gently.

James swallowed down some of the whisky in his glass, and some of the colour returned to his cheeks. 'I needed that!' He closed his eyes briefly before turning to look at her. 'It's a shock to see you, Ellie,' he admitted gruffly. 'And here, of all places.'

She raised auburn brows. 'Surely Daniel told you he had been to the hotel?'

'Well . . . yes. But he didn't say— Well, I had no idea the two of you had become this friendly.' He frowned darkly.

The same age as herself, James was an attractive man; his hair was dark, and slightly overlong at the moment, and his blue shirt and fitted denims suited his slightly leaner frame. Ellie had always thought the two of them got on quite well together, but she could see that at the moment James wished himself any-where but in her company; perhaps that had some-thing to do with the other woman in his life that Beth had told her about. Although the fact that James looked so physically awful must mean that he still cared for Beth—very much so, if his reaction to just the sound of her name was anything to go by.

'Daniel and I haven't become "friendly", James,' Ellie assured him drily. 'The only reason I'm here to-night is because I was hoping he could tell me where I might find you. Obviously he could have done so!' Days ago, she acknowledged, somewhat angrily.

'I asked him not to,' James admitted flatly.

Ellie frowned at him. 'But surely Daniel must have told you how ill Beth looks?' she admonished abruptly. 'That she asked him about you?'

'Yes, he told me,' James acknowledged heavily.

'And?'

He gave a deep sigh. 'As far as I can see, nothing has changed, Ellie. Hell, the fact that you're the one who's here proves that!' He scowled.

Ellie frowned, shaking her head. 'I don't understand, James.'

He gave an embittered smile. 'You never did.'

She gently touched his arm. 'Then tell me,' she encouraged. 'Help me to understand why it is that two people, who obviously love each other very much, have been apart for the last month.' She shook her head. 'Because I certainly don't understand that!'

James frowned. 'What has Beth told you?'

Only a garbled story about another woman—and Ellie still had a problem believing that. Besides, it wouldn't be a very good start to their conversation if James thought she was accusing him of something...

'Very little,' Ellie told him truthfully. 'One day you were at the hotel and the next you weren't—and Beth was in no mood at the time to give explanations about anything. She still isn't!' Ellie grimaced as she thought of her stubborn sister.

James drew in a deeply ragged breath. 'How is she really, Ellie? Daniel said she didn't look too good last week, but what the hell does that really mean? I don't—'

'Let's sit down, James,' she suggested softly. 'We may as well be comfortable while we talk.' Besides, the way James was drinking whisky, he might just fall down if he didn't soon sit down. And if they both sat down it wouldn't feel as if James was about to turn on his heel and leave at any moment. Even if he was!

He sat down after a moment's hesitation, nursing his half-full glass between both his hands as he sat forward in the chair, staring down at the brown contents, his expression completely morose.

'What are you doing now, James?' Ellie prompted. 'Are you working?' He had been so capable at helping them manage the hotel.

'Yes,' he answered abruptly.

'What are you doing?' she asked interestedly.

'Look, I thought we were going to talk about Beth.' He cut across her line of questioning. 'You said you would tell me how she is.' He scowled across at her.

'Beth is awful; how did you expect her to be?' Ellie raised auburn brows at him.

'Oh, God . . .!' He sank back in the seat, closing his eyes briefly.

'James, tell me what's wrong,' she encouraged earnestly. 'Maybe I can help.'

A bitter laugh greeted this comment, and James looked across at her with scorn in his gaze. What was so funny about her offering to help? She didn't—

'That's ironic.' James shook his head derisively. 'Very ironic. When it's—' He broke off as they both heard the sound of a key in the lock of the front door.

Daniel was home. Only just over the promised hour, Ellie inwardly acknowledged after a brief glance at her wristwatch. But she could only wish that he had been longer; she doubted James was going to talk to her with the other man present.

'I told you I wouldn't be too late—' Daniel broke off his mocking remark as he entered the room— alone—and saw James seated there with Ellie. 'Ah.' He seemed to take in the situation at a glance, turning to James after giving Ellie a briefly challenging look. 'Good to see you again, James.' He held out his hand in greeting to the other man.

'Daniel.' James returned the greeting abruptly. 'Ellie and I have been—talking.'

Daniel put down his briefcase and poured himself a measure of whisky into a glass. 'About anything interesting?' he enquired casually as he sat down in one of the leather armchairs.

Very interesting, as far as Ellie was concerned; she had just been about to find out the reason why James had left Beth so abruptly! But with Daniel's arrival back she had a feeling her brother-in-law would clam up again. Although Daniel was obviously aware of James's reason for going...

'Not really,' James dismissed tersely, standing up in a restless movement. 'I didn't need to see you about anything important, Daniel, so I'll leave the two of you to enjoy your evening—'

'You damn well won't leave us,' Daniel told him decisively. 'Ellie and I were just about to make dinner—you can join us.' He said the last in such a tone that it was an order, not an invitation.

Ellie stared across at Daniel; they were going to 'make' dinner? It was the first she had heard of it! She had assumed— incorrectly, it now turned out!— that the two of them would be going out to eat. Thank God James had turned up so unexpectedly; the last thing Ellie wanted was to share a meal alone with Daniel in the intimacy of his apartment!

James looked unconvinced, despite the other man's tone. 'I don't think—'

'No, James, I don't think you've been doing that for some time,' Daniel cut in softly. 'Let's all cook dinner, and then maybe we can thrash this thing out between the three of us. Ellie has taken the trouble to come here, James—to see you, as it happens,' he continued as the other man would have protested again. 'The least you can do is be hospitable,' he added in hard challenge, his gaze compelling.

James looked at him mutinously for several long seconds, and then he slowly nodded. 'OK,' he finally conceded. 'But I don't see what you hope to achieve.'

'*I* don't hope to achieve anything, James,' Daniel put in derisively. 'It's your marriage that seems to be at stake here. I presume you *do* want to try to salvage something from it?' he added harshly.

James seemed to wilt visibly, his face haggard, his eyes haunted. 'You know I do,' he muttered.

'Then accept the invitation, eat some food, and then maybe tempers will have cooled somewhat,' Daniel said grimly.

As far as Ellie was concerned, she didn't have a temper to cool. She was still vaguely puzzled by her earlier conversation with James, and that was her primary feeling. And it seemed that that puzzlement wasn't to be alleviated until after dinner. Hopefully, she would get some answers then ...

It was a very strange experience being in Daniel's luxurious kitchen—where every conceivable modern appliance seemed to be located somewhere amongst its fitted walnut units—as the two of them prepared the meal. James seemed to be spending most of his time sitting at the kitchen table helping himself to the bottle of red wine Daniel had opened in preparation for accompanying the steaks they were now cooking.

'How long has he been like this?' Ellie asked Daniel quietly as James refilled his wine glass.

Daniel gave his friend a brief glance. 'Weeks,' he admitted grimly. 'Now you know why I decided to come to your hotel myself; I could have quite easily sent a junior to speak to Osborne,' he dismissed drily. 'I wanted to see for myself exactly what was going on there.'

'And?'

He shrugged. 'We'll talk later, Ellie.'

When Daniel decided they would, she realised frustratedly. He was certainly a man who liked to be in charge, but the way this situation was at the moment she had no other choice than to let him be. It wasn't

easy fighting down that stubbornly independent side
of her nature, but for the moment she was managing
to do it; after all, she had got her wish—she was going
to talk to James later on. If he was sober enough to
do any talking by then, she acknowledged with a
rueful shake of her head as James again emptied his
wine glass of the ruby-red wine.

'Prepare the salad, Ellie,' Daniel instructed hardily
as he easily followed the direction of her gaze. 'The
sooner we all eat, the better it will be, I think,' he
added grimly.

Daniel proved to be a very capable chef. Not in
Peter's league, of course, but nevertheless the steak
was cooked to perfection, and so too were the accompanying mushrooms and onions—and the dressing
he'd prepared for the salad tasted like nothing Ellie
had ever eaten.

'A secret recipe,' he told her as he saw her obvious
enjoyment.

'You should bottle it and sell it; you would make
a fortune!' she told him without hesitation.

'Make a note of this, James,' he told his friend drily.
'It's the first compliment Ellie has ever given me.
No—don't spoil it,' he said as she would have spoken.
'I'm more than well aware it's probably the last time
too!' He looked across at her with mocking blue eyes.

'I was going to say it's the first time you've de-
served one!' she corrected waspishly.

Daniel burst into throaty laughter, looking at her
appreciatively. 'You're an amazing woman, Ellie. The
only woman, I believe, who has ever made me annoyed, angry, filled with desire and then made me

laugh, all within a very short space of time!' He shook his head in self-derision.

'Maybe you should marry her!' James put in insultingly, having eaten little of his own meal, despite their best efforts to get him to do so.

Daniel frowned across at his friend, his eyes narrowed to steely slits. 'Maybe I should,' he finally said slowly, holding James's gaze in challenge. 'She isn't at all the woman you led me to believe she was,' he added harshly.

Ellie frowned at the two of them; she'd had no idea the two of them had ever discussed what sort of woman she was. When had this conversation taken place? Before Daniel had come to the hotel, or since his return to London?

James stood up abruptly, pushing his chair back noisily. 'So she has you fooled too now, does she?' he scorned disgustedly, his words slightly slurred. 'Well, I may as well give up and go home—'

'Sit down, James,' Daniel instructed softly—but nevertheless the steel was audible in his voice.

'But—'

'I said sit down, James.' He hadn't moved, was still perfectly relaxed in his chair, but at the same time he gave the impression of a leashed animal about to spring—and if James made another move to leave that was exactly what he was likely to do! 'Before you fall down,' he added forcefully.

James sank back into his chair like a deflated balloon. 'The two of you seem very close,' he muttered accusingly.

Ellie was still stunned by the exchange. Most of James's anger seemed to be directed at her—and she had no idea why!

'Not as close as I would like,' Daniel told his friend grimly. 'But maybe that can be rectified once we've sorted this mess out.' He turned questioningly to Ellie.

She was totally lost by the conversation now. How could she and Daniel possibly become close? The man was getting married at the weekend!

'I don't believe this!' James stood up again, a defiant expression on his face this time. 'After all that I've told you, all the things—'

'Don't you think you could have been slightly biased in your interpretation of those "things"?' Daniel prompted softly.

James's mouth twisted disgustedly. 'I seem to be the one who's been living in London the last month without my wife!'

Daniel shrugged. 'That appears to have been your choice.'

James moved noisily away from the table. 'This is incredible!' he said disbelievingly, speaking to no one in particular—himself probably, he was so lost in his own drink-induced misery by this time.

'For I don't know how long I put up with "We'll have to cancel the wedding because Ellie can't be there." "No, we can't go off on holiday and leave Ellie on her own." "No, we can't make any changes at the hotel without first discussing them with Ellie." "No, you can't take a job somewhere else, because that wouldn't be fair on Ellie." Fair!' James turned to glare furiously across the room at her. 'Beth was married to *me*, Ellie, not you—although no one would have thought that when she always put your welfare above mine or that of our marriage!'

Ellie gaped at him, her face having gone paler and paler as James had seemed to spit the words angrily at her. She had had no idea that there was so much resentment below the surface—directed at her from James.

After a brief glance at her stunned expression Daniel stood up abruptly, facing the other man, seeming almost to stand defensively in front of Ellie. 'That's enough, James—'

'Of course it isn't enough,' the other man scorned. 'It isn't nearly enough! I...' James didn't so much break off as fade away, his whole body seeming to suddenly deflate before he sank slowly to the floor.

Daniel looked down at him dispassionately. 'Drunk,' he said disgustedly.

Ellie hadn't moved, couldn't move. Because as James had let loose his tirade at her a sudden realisation had come to her; *she* was the 'other woman' in James's life that Beth had told her about... *She* was the reason her sister's marriage had broken up!

CHAPTER NINE

'I DON'T think you should take too much notice of the ramblings of a drunken man,' Daniel advised, his expression grim as he looked at the paleness of her face.

Ellie shook her head. 'James wasn't rambling.' She spoke flatly. 'And he wasn't saying anything that you hadn't heard before.' She looked up accusingly at Daniel. 'You knew he thought those things about me,' she continued brokenly, standing up abruptly. 'I can't believe it!' She shook her head again. 'All this time I thought— I didn't know—' Her voice broke emotionally as she turned away, not wanting Daniel to see her complete breakdown, tears flooding her vision.

'Ellie—'

'Don't touch me!' Her eyes flashed deeply green as she turned on him, her arms wrapped protectively about herself. 'You came to the hotel last week believing—believing—'

Daniel reached out towards her, but his arms fell back against his sides as he saw the way she recoiled from his touch. 'I don't believe it any longer,' he assured her huskily.

Her head went back challengingly. 'No? Exactly what happened to change your mind, Daniel?' she scorned. 'You—' She broke off as James gave a drink-induced groan and looked down impatiently at her brother-in-law. 'Nothing James said, obviously!' she bit out tautly.

'I suggest we get James into bed and let him sleep this off,' Daniel said grimly. 'Then we can talk properly.'

'There's nothing to talk about. Not between the two of us, anyway,' Ellie dismissed coldly.

'I don't agree with you.' Daniel shook his head.

'I really don't give a damn what you think,' she told him bluntly. 'And there will be no talking to James tonight either, from the look of him,' she acknowledged derisively. Her brother-in-law was out cold now, slumped right down in the chair. 'If you would direct me to the appropriate bedroom . . .?' She bent down to begin pulling James up onto his feet.

Daniel looked at her wordlessly for several moments, and then took the bulk of James's weight onto his own shoulders. 'James is drunk, Ellie,' he told her softly as they walked James towards one of the bedrooms. 'Very drunk. And when he sobers up in the morning he's going to regret that he said as much as he did.' This last was added grimly—as if Daniel intended making sure that James was sorry—very sorry!

She shook her head dismissively. 'From the little he has said I believe someone should have spoken sooner.' Much sooner! James's resentment towards her had obviously started even before he and Beth were married, and it had got worse, not better.

Although having listened to his 'ramblings', she couldn't exactly say that she blamed him for feeling the way he did; her only excuse was that she had had no idea how much Beth had put what she'd believed were her sister's wishes before those of her husband.

If she had known she wouldn't have allowed it. But she hadn't known, and it seemed to have seriously damaged Beth and James's marriage. Not irrevocably, she hoped...

She barely noticed the decor in the bedroom Daniel took them to, only registered enough in the lemon and cream room to know that from the complete lack of personal effects this wasn't Daniel's own bedroom. They laid their heavy burden down on top of the lemon-coloured duvet. James was still not stirring, although his loud breathing sounded as if it precluded snoring.

Daniel impatiently pulled off the other man's shoes and covered him haphazardly with the duvet.

Ellie frowned. 'Shouldn't we make him more comfortable? Take off his clothes or something?' She grimaced inadequately.

'In other circumstances, possibly,' Daniel dismissed uninterestedly. 'In these circumstances, he's lucky we've even put him on the bed.' He turned to leave the room without giving James so much as a second look.

After a regretful glance at her brother-in-law, Ellie had little choice but to follow Daniel, closing the bedroom door softly behind her. Not that she thought for a moment that she might disturb James; it was going to be hours before he regained consciousness—and, at a guess, he was going to have the headache to end all headaches when he did!

'Let's have a cup of coffee,' Daniel suggested grimly once she had rejoined him in the sitting room. 'I think enough wine has been consumed here already tonight.'

She had no interest in drinking wine, or coffee, or anything else for that matter. She shook her head. 'I think I would rather just leave—'

'To go where?' He looked at her with narrowed eyes.

'I booked into a hotel before coming here this evening,' she told him distractedly; it was almost eleven o'clock now—hardly the time to arrive at a hotel. Although this was London, of course, and some people didn't even go out until this time of night. But not Ellie; she wanted to get a good night's sleep before going back home tomorrow. The sooner she talked to Beth about this tangled mess the better. For everyone's sake!

'Very efficient,' Daniel said drily. 'You had no intention of staying here, then?' He quirked dark brows at her.

She frowned across at him. Why on earth—? 'Certainly not!' she snapped impatiently as his meaning became clear.

He shrugged. 'Just an idea. We wouldn't have been interrupted here—as we seem to have been so many times before.'

It wasn't that many times she had been in his arms—and she wished he wouldn't remind her of them!

Ellie shook her head disgustedly. 'You already have a house-guest for the night. Not your usual gender, I'm sure,' she added waspishly, 'but I'm afraid, as far as I'm concerned, it will have to do!'

'Let's call a truce for a while, Ellie.' All the banter had left Daniel now, and there was a weary expression on his face as he ran a hand through the dark thickness of his hair. 'A cup of coffee isn't going to 'hurt you,' he added heavily. 'And God knows it's been a traumatic enough evening!'

Ellie was the one to move about the kitchen preparing the coffee, having found everything necessary earlier, when she had been left here on her own. 'Didn't your business meeting go well?' she asked curiously as she poured the coffee.

'Business meeting...?' For a moment Daniel looked confused by the question, and then his brow cleared. 'Oh, that went fine—as I had no doubt it would!' he dismissed easily.

Her brows quirked. 'Another successful takeover bid?' she derided, sitting on the bar-stool beside him as they drank their coffee.

He frowned again, looking at her over the rim of his mug for several seconds, then finally sitting back in his seat. 'You don't like me very much, do you, Ellie?' he said slowly, as if the idea had only just occurred to him—and he didn't like it very much!

It wasn't a question of liking or not liking him— she was more attracted to him than it could possibly be safe to be. To be attracted to him at all, considering the other female complications in his life, was pure madness on her part!

Of course she liked him. She loved—Ellie abruptly halted her thoughts on that word. Love? She didn't love Daniel Thackery! Did she...?

'What's the matter, Ellie?' He frowned his concern at the sudden paleness of her cheeks. 'Look, James is out of his head with drink, so don't take too much notice of what he said earlier.'

Daniel rose to stand beside her as she sat on the bar-stool, his arm moving protectively about her shoulders. 'God, he's going to regret this in the morning,' he muttered, the look he shot towards the bedroom where James lay seeming to say that he would make sure the other man damn well regretted it! 'Ellie, don't look like that!' Daniel groaned, bending his head down towards her.

This shouldn't be happening, was Ellie's last thought, and yet as Daniel's mouth claimed hers, gently at first, and then more fiercely, she knew that it was what she craved the most, what she most needed.

Daniel's fierceness evaporated as he felt her response—her lips soft and pliant beneath his, her body moulded against the hardness of his as he pulled her effortlessly to her feet. His mouth was softly exploring now, his heartbeat a loud tattoo against her breasts.

It was always like this between them, she acknowledged with an inward groan, and her legs seemed to melt beneath her as Daniel's hand lightly cupped one of her breasts, his lips still plundering her own, the tip of his tongue dipping moistly into her mouth, telling her that he wanted her as much as she wanted him.

But she already knew that, could feel the pulsing hardness of his thighs against her, his heart beating even more rapidly beneath her hand as she clung to him for support—a support he seemed only too ready to give as his thumbtip moved rhythmically over the hardened nub of her breast.

Fire instantly warmed her body, an uncontrollable heat that coursed through her veins from the top of her head to the tips of her toes.

'I want you, Ellie,' Daniel groaned against the warmth of her throat. 'I want to make love to you until neither of us can think straight!'

She was already at that stage, with no thought of denial in her head as she looked up at him with darkened green eyes. She loved this man—loved him with a passion that allowed no thought for anything else.

Daniel cupped each side of her face as he looked deeply into her eyes. 'Stay with me tonight, Ellie,' he pleaded throatily. 'Stay with me, and I promise you won't regret it!'

Oh, yes, she would—more than he could ever know. But at this moment in time she didn't care. She just didn't care!

'Oh, Daniel, I—' She broke off as there was a loud thumping noise from somewhere else in the apartment. For a moment she was totally dazed by the interruption, and then there was a crashing noise of something breaking. 'James!' she gasped in realisation.

'Goddamn—!' Daniel openly cursed the interruption, reluctant to release his hold on her. 'Ellie—'

'He could have hurt himself,' she reasoned quickly, her expression anxious.

'He deserves to have broken his damned neck!' Daniel said grimly, not even a hint of concern in his furious expression.

Ellie pulled out of his arms. 'He's your friend, Daniel.' She frowned.

'He's a damned mess, is what he is—'

'Swearing isn't going to help,' she murmured distractedly as she heard another thumping sound from the direction of the bedroom they had left James in.

'It makes me feel better!' Daniel rasped angrily, turning to stride impatiently from the kitchen, pausing to turn in the doorway to face her. 'Don't leave, Ellie,' he requested gruffly.

She had no intention of leaving—yet. Although, as he had probably correctly guessed, she would be doing so once she had ascertained that James hadn't injured himself. The moment of intimacy between Daniel and herself was irrevocably broken. It should never have begun!

She had learned tonight—devastatingly—that she was the reason behind the break-up of Beth and James's marriage, and the last thing she needed was to get physically involved with a man who was about to be married to someone else.

'Damn him!' Daniel muttered grimly as he read her answer in her face. 'At least talk to me before you leave,' he said frustratedly.

They had nothing to say. She had almost made another mistake tonight. The last of many, it seemed... But the others she could rectify—she hoped. Going to bed with Daniel would be beyond mending. For herself. And she already had enough to deal with at the moment, without adding to her problems. And her feelings for Daniel were certainly a problem. She only hoped she could learn to deal with them once she was safely away from here—and him!

He heaved a deep sigh at her uncompromising expression. 'Whatever you may think to the contrary, Ellie, we do have to talk—'

'Not now, we don't.' Her voice was gruff as she finally spoke. 'James is much more important.'

'I don't happen to think so,' Daniel muttered grimly. 'But I can see you don't agree with me.' He shook his head disgustedly as he turned to lead the way to the lemon and cream bedroom where they had left James earlier.

James had obviously woken, and had knocked the bedside lamp to the floor and broken it as he'd tried to get up. He was crawling around on the carpet at the moment, trying to get back up onto his feet.

'Where the hell do you think you're going?' Daniel demanded harshly as he helped the other man up into a sitting position on the bed.

'I feel ill,' James groaned, his face seeming to have a green tinge to it as he looked up at Daniel. 'In fact, I think I'm going to—'

'Bathroom. Quickly!' Ellie instructed hurriedly as she could see the imminent onset of nausea.

They just managed, between the two of them— James himself being absolutely no help whatsoever— to get him into the adjoining bathroom before he was violently ill.

Daniel looked at the other man in disgust. 'I think you should go and wait in the bedroom,' he advised Ellie distractedly. 'No reason why both of us should be subjected to this,' he added grimly as the other man continued to be sick.

Ellie didn't need a second telling; she had never been at her best around people who were being physically ill in the way that James now was.

She used the time to tidy the kitchen, where they had eaten their meal. She would have liked to just leave before Daniel returned, but she didn't feel that would be particularly fair to him; James might be his friend but he was *her* brother-in-law.

'How is he?' She turned to Daniel as he re-entered the kitchen a few minutes later.

He still looked grim. 'Out cold again. Although I doubt he'll wake up again this time; he's been so ill he must be absolutely exhausted!'

'It has to stop, you know.' Ellie frowned. 'James can't go on like that any more than Beth can continue in her stressed-out state.'

'You're right about James.' Daniel nodded abruptly. 'I had no idea he was as near the edge as this. God knows, there have been complaints from the staff, but—'

'What staff?' she put in sharply, looking at him with narrowed eyes.

He gave a heavy sigh. 'I suppose this is something else you aren't aware of,' he muttered grimly. 'James has been working for me for the last month, Ellie,' he informed her abruptly. 'As manager in a hotel I acquired several months ago.'

She stiffened. So the suspicions they had had about his interest in buying into hotels hadn't been so far wrong after all... It was just a little out of date; Daniel had already begun doing so—and he had employed James to work in one!

'And did you offer him this job before or after he left Beth?' She looked at him challengingly.

His mouth firmed at her accusing tone. 'Before, of course. But—'

'And you had the nerve to accuse *me* of being manipulative!' Ellie scorned, shaking her head derisively.

'Beth wouldn't leave the hotel because of you!' Daniel pointed out exasperatedly.

'That may be true, Daniel,' she acknowledged with a nod, sure that it was—although it was a situation she intended rectifying with her sister as soon as she returned home. 'But you were obviously aware of the problems James was having with his marriage when you made him the job offer, which means you aren't completely innocent in this either,' she told him sharply.

'I never said I was,' he rasped impatiently.

'You didn't say a lot of things.' Her eyes flashed deeply green. 'The most important of them being that you knew exactly where James was all the time!' She shook her head disgustedly. 'I have to go, Daniel,' she told him wearily, picking up her handbag in preparation. 'When James wakes up in the morning could you tell him to expect to hear from Beth very soon?'

She didn't care how stubbornly her sister was avoiding meeting James—she intended making Beth at least talk to him and try to sort this mess out. Most of all, she intended making it absolutely clear to her sister that she was not the 'other woman' in their marriage, and that Beth's place was with her husband.

'We need to talk, Ellie—'

'We don't need to do anything, Daniel.' She shot him a fiercely warning look, feeling close to screaming if she didn't soon get out of here.

It had been a traumatic evening—even more so than she had originally envisaged. It had been a tremendous shock to her to realise that she had been the stumbling block in her sister's marriage all the time—but even more of a shock to suddenly realise that she had fallen in love with Daniel Thackery, a man destined to marry another woman within a matter of days! What a disaster!

'Just pass my message on to James when he wakes up,' she said abruptly.

'Ellie—'

'I said we have nothing more to say to each other, Daniel!' she told him sharply as he would have reached out to her, willing him to realise just how close to breaking point she actually was; she had to get away without further delay.

His jaw clenched as he obviously fought down the urge to continue arguing the point with her. 'I'll drive you to your hotel,' he finally bit out grimly.

'No—'

'Yes, Ellie!' he grated harshly, a nerve pulsing in his rigidly set cheek.

'James—'

'Isn't going to come to any harm during the short time it will take me to drive you to your hotel,' Daniel insisted dismissively. 'I certainly don't intend staying awake all night wet-nursing him—in fact, my days of patience where he's concerned are over!'

From the harshly determined expression on his face, Ellie didn't think too much of James's chances of escaping the wrath of Daniel's cutting tongue once the other man was sober. But that was between Daniel and James; she had her own situation with her sister to sort out.

Daniel was grimly silent on the drive to Ellie's hotel, and, as Ellie had nothing to say either, she was glad when the short journey was over.

'Thank—'

'Don't thank me, Ellie.' He cut into the politeness of her words once they reached the hotel. 'You have nothing to thank me for!'

She gave a dismissive shrug, turning to get out of the car, reluctantly half turning back to him as he put a restraining hand on her arm.

'I'll be in touch, Ellie,' he told her huskily, his gaze searching on the paleness of her face.

She had no intention of seeing him again, and certainly not once he was married to Angela. 'Don't bother, Daniel,' she said curtly, getting out of the car. 'With Beth gone I'm going to be too busy looking after the hotel in future to have time for anything else.'

'You seem pretty sure you'll be able to persuade Beth to go.' He frowned.

'Contrary to what everyone else seems to think,' Ellie returned scornfully, 'I believe Beth's place is with her husband.' And their baby, she added silently.

And hopefully the amount of work she would have to do once she was on her own at the hotel would keep her too busy to be able even to think of Daniel!

'And is Osborne included in this being too busy to have time for anything else?' Daniel taunted harshly.

She stiffened defensively at his mention of the other man, remembering all too vividly the accusations he had made to her concerning Peter. 'That's between Peter and myself,' she told him coldly, having no intention of explaining herself, or Peter, to this man. Besides, the things Peter had told her about his private life he had told her in confidence; it wasn't for her to break that.

Daniel's mouth twisted. 'I see.' He straightened in his seat. 'There's one thing I believe you should think about, though, Ellie: you wouldn't respond to me in the way that you do if you were in love with Osborne,' he told her challengingly.

She had realised tonight exactly who she was in love with—and it wasn't Peter! 'Goodnight, Daniel!' She slammed the car door shut behind her and walked up the steps to the hotel, her head held proudly erect.

There was no way she wanted Daniel to know just how traumatic this evening had been for her. In more ways than one!

But once she was inside the foyer of the hotel her shoulders drooped and she felt all the fight leave her. It had been a terrible evening, one of the worst she could ever remember.

And the whole sorry mess was far from over yet.

'James had no right to tell you anything!' Beth snapped, her eyes flashing defiantly.

Ellie had driven back to their hotel the following morning, the evidence of her almost sleepless night in the dark shadows beneath her eyes and the hollows in her cheeks. She had paused only long enough to deposit her overnight case in their sitting room before seeking Beth out in the office.

Despite having wanted to hear news of James, Beth was far from pleased, once she knew what he'd had to say, at Ellie having seen him in London.

Ellie shook her head. 'Don't you think it was time someone did?' she prompted softly.

Beth looked rebellious. 'James's opinion is biased—'

'James knows how he feels, Beth,' she quietly interrupted. 'And to be honest, now that I know the truth about the last year or so, I can't exactly blame him! You didn't even tell me that James had been offered another job, let alone that he wanted to take it and for the two of you to move to London,' she added with gentle accusation.

Beth couldn't quite meet her gaze. 'I didn't see the point in talking to you about it. We couldn't go and that was the end of the subject. There is no way you can manage here on your own— '

'Who says I can't?' Ellie raised darkly auburn brows.

'Of course you can't, Ellie,' her sister dismissed impatiently. 'We both know how hard the two of us have to work to keep the place going—if one of us just disappeared that would be totally unfair to the other one.'

She shrugged. 'That used to be true, yes . . .'

Beth looked puzzled. 'Surely it still is . . .?'

'Perhaps if I intended remaining here on my own, yes,' she returned lightly. 'But you're taking an awful lot for granted in assuming that's what I'm going to do.'

She had thought about this long and hard the night before, and had decided that the best way to deal with this was to show Beth that she could manage perfectly well—both privately and in business—without her. And she had come to the conclusion that there was only one way for Beth to believe that. She only hoped Peter wouldn't mind her using their friendship in this way!

Her sister's cheeks had flushed at her slightly mocking tone. 'I don't understand.' She shook her head.

'It's quite simple really, Beth,' Ellie said pointedly. 'I don't intend being here on my own.'

'We can't afford to pay a manager to help—'

'Beth,' she cut in exasperatedly, 'I wasn't talking about a manager! Just exactly what is it I've done to give you the impression I intend spending the rest of my life as an old maid? Or is it that you consider I'm so unattractive—' she frowned '— that no one will want me?'

'Of course not,' her sister answered protestingly. 'You've just never given the impression— Well, you've always—' She broke off awkwardly. 'I just assumed—'

'Don't assume anything where I'm concerned, Beth,' she cut in sharply, knowing she had to be cruel to be kind. 'But especially don't assume that I intend the two of us to spend the rest of our days together running this hotel, ending up as the spinster sisters who never had a life of their own!'

'I didn't think that...' Beth trailed off lamely. 'You've always looked after me, Ellie,' she continued huskily, her blue eyes wide. 'Especially so since Mummy and Daddy moved to Spain. I just thought— I shouldn't have done, I realise that now.' She shook her head. 'I've made such a mess of things!' she realised with a groan.

'It isn't too late to do something about it,' Ellie assured her softly. 'James still loves you—although after some of the stunts you've pulled over the last year I'm not sure you deserve it!' she added chidingly.

Tears filled the dark blue eyes. 'I never wanted to let you down.' Beth sighed shakily.

'So you let James down instead.' She shook her head. 'He's your husband, Beth, and as such he should come first. And now that the two of you are expecting a baby you have that to think about too. I'm going to be just fine,' she assured her lightly.

Her sister looked at her curiously. 'Who's the lucky man, Ellie? Or shouldn't I ask?'

She had known this question would come, and she was ready for it. 'Not yet,' she answered coyly. 'I'm not too sure he knows himself yet,' she added teasingly.

'Peter?' Beth guessed excitedly. 'It has to be Peter!'

Because he was the only man Ellie had so much as been out to dinner with over the last few years! Strange—she and Daniel had never actually been out together, and yet she had somehow managed to fall in love with him . . .

'I told you, I'm not saying,' Ellie dismissed firmly. 'Besides, we have much more important things to sort out at the moment—things like you going to James and apologising to him.' She looked pointedly at her sister.

Beth's cheeks were flushed. 'I—'

'I'm sorry, but after what's happened you have to be the one to go to him, Beth,' she cut in softly. 'You really can't expect him to come crawling back here when you are the one in the wrong.' She intended leaving her sister in no doubt that that was what she believed; there had to be no room for doubt. And Beth and James had to get back together, as quickly as possible, for everyone's benefit.

Beth's eyes were huge now in the paleness of her face. 'I don't know if I'll be able to—'

'I don't think you can do anything else,' Ellie told
her decisively.

Her sister shook her head. 'I was going to say I
don't know if I'll be able to find him; he seems to
have done a very good disappearing act!' She grimaced ruefully.

'He was staying at Daniel Thackery's apartment last
night.' She decided it was probably best not to mention
the circumstances under which James had been forced
to accept the other man's hospitality! 'And if he's left
there now—' which, in all likelihood, he would have,
as it was now almost eleven o'clock in the morning
'—I'm sure Daniel will be only too happy to tell you
where you can find him.'

Her sister didn't look convinced. 'He wasn't too
helpful in that direction last time!'

'Daniel has had a change of heart since then,' Ellie
assured her. She was absolutely positive that he wanted
James's private life sorted out as badly as she did now;
a drunken manager in his hotel was not, she was sure,
Daniel's idea of a good situation.

Beth still looked undecided. 'What if James doesn't
want to see me?'

'He—' She broke off as the sound of raised voices
could be heard out in the reception area, standing up
just as James came bursting into the room.

He looked little better than he had last night—in
fact, on closer inspection, he was still wearing the same
clothes he had been wearing then, and they looked
even more disreputable than they had before.
Probably because they had literally been slept in! His
hair was standing up on end, as if he had been running

his fingers through it for hours—which he probably had, judging by the haggard expression on his face.

Ellie turned to look at a now seriously shaken Beth. 'Well, I think you have the answer to your last question,' she said drily.

Beth swallowed hard, a mixture of emotions on her face—excitement at seeing James again, but also apprehension at what the outcome of their conversation might be. 'I—'

'I think we should leave the two of them alone to talk, don't you?' Daniel suddenly remarked pointedly.

Ellie had had no idea he was there until he'd spoken, hadn't seen him standing behind the other man. And, now that she had seen him, she wondered what on earth he was doing here...

CHAPTER TEN

'JAMES may be basically sober now, but I was sure a blood test would show he was still way over the limit for driving himself here,' Daniel supplied drily when Ellie put her question to him a few minutes later. The two of them were sitting in one of the lounges, having left Beth and James alone in the office.

He certainly had a point; judging by the amount of alcohol she had seen James consume the evening before, it wouldn't have just disappeared from his system overnight.

'He *has* come to sort things out with Beth, hasn't he?' A worrying thought had suddenly occurred to her. She had assumed that was what her brother-in-law was here for, but if it wasn't...

'He had better.' Daniel's expression was grim. 'Otherwise he's going to be minus a wife, a job and a friend,' he added harshly.

And a baby, she could have added—but it was for Beth to tell that news, not Ellie—not to anyone. 'I hope you haven't put any pressure on him.' She frowned. 'Because if he doesn't really want to be here—'

'What do you think, Ellie?' Daniel cut in impatiently, sitting forward in his armchair. 'Did he act last night like a man who enjoys being without his wife?'

No, of course he hadn't. But James and Beth already seemed to have made such a mess of things between them that the last thing they needed now was to be together for the wrong reasons.

'James was determined to come down here today, Ellie,' Daniel continued exasperatedly as she still didn't look convinced. 'I merely offered, in the circumstances, to be his chauffeur!'

'I—'

'I believe the two of you ordered coffee,' remarked a familiar voice, and Ellie looked up to smile at Peter as he put down the tray of coffee things on the table in front of them; she had almost forgotten that she had telephoned through to the kitchen a few minutes ago to order coffee for Daniel and herself.

'Does the chef of the hotel usually bring out coffee for guests himself?' Daniel asked sharply, giving the other man a coldly hard look.

Peter grinned, not at all abashed by the other man's obvious mockery. 'When he knows it's for Ellie, yes!' He gave her a warm smile.

'I see,' Daniel bit out with obvious displeasure, his eyes icily blue. 'Well, you've delivered it,' he added pointedly.

Ellie gasped at his rudeness, although Peter looked completely unconcerned.

'How are you, Ellie?' Peter enquired lightly, ignoring the other man. 'Did you enjoy your couple of days away?'

'I—'

'Could the two of you continue this polite conversation at some other time?' Daniel cut in harshly, a nerve pulsing in his rigidly held jaw. 'Ellie and I were in the middle of a discussion.' He looked at the other man challengingly.

'Sorry I interrupted,' Peter told him dismissively, the wink he shot at Ellie as he turned to leave telling her that he knew exactly what he was doing—and that far from being insulted by the other man's arrogant attitude he was actually enjoying himself!

She shook her head at this display of childishness from both men; maybe it was true, after all, that men never actually grew up. Well, she certainly hoped that James had, and that he and her sister managed to sort out their differences!

'Well, are you going to pour the coffee or do you want me to do it?' Daniel suddenly rasped. 'Sorry,' he muttered as she looked across at him with pointedly raised brows. 'I didn't have a very good night.' He ran an agitated hand through the dark thickness of his hair.

She poured the coffee, smiling slightly. 'I thought you said you weren't going to run around after James all night,' she reminded him teasingly, unaware that she had automatically added milk but no sugar to his coffee before handing it to him.

Daniel took the cup. 'My sleepless night had nothing to do with James.' He sounded disgruntled.

Ellie frowned, looking across at him, slowly becoming aware, from the way he met her gaze so steadily, that she had had something to do with his sleepless night. But why? Because she hadn't stayed the night with him at the apartment as he had hoped? Only his arrogance could have led him to believe for one moment that she might have done! Or maybe it was the fact that he had asked her to stay with him that had bothered him after she had left...?

'A guilty conscience has a way of keeping one awake,' she acknowledged frostily. After all, he was due to marry Angela at the weekend.

'Guilty...?' Daniel frowned. 'But I—'

'Oh, Ellie, it's going to be all right!' Beth came bursting into the room, the radiant expression on her face telling its own story. 'James and I have talked, and—well, it's going to be all right!' she repeated excitedly.

Ellie stood up to hug her sister. 'I'm so glad,' she said throatily, pleased to see her sister looking happy at last. 'For both of you.' She turned to include a still rather shamefaced James in the warmth of her smile.

'Does this mean I'm going to get a competent hotel manager, after all?' Daniel put in drily, also standing up.

James swallowed hard. 'I—'

'I was only teasing you, James,' the other man interrupted mockingly, holding out his hand. 'Even working at half your potential you're still the best damned hotel manager I've ever had.'

James returned the other man's handshake, his mouth twisting wryly at the compliment. 'I'm the only hotel manager you've ever had!'

Daniel grinned. 'True,' he drawled derisively. 'But I would guess Ellie is going to miss the two of you around here.' He looked at her with narrowed eyes.

But Ellie was ready for him, her expression deliberately unconcerned as she returned his gaze. She had told him she only wanted Beth's happiness, and that still held true, and she didn't want him even to begin to think otherwise. Yes, it was going to be difficult running the hotel on her own, but she would manage somehow. She would have to!

'The three of us,' James announced proudly, putting his arm protectively about Beth's shoulders as he pulled her closer to his side. 'Beth and I are expecting a baby,' he told the other man, his excitement at the prospect of becoming a father there in his voice for them all to hear.

'That's wonderful,' Daniel told them warmly, looking questioningly at Ellie.

She gave a barely perceptible nod, letting him know that she had been aware of Beth's condition well before this moment.

'And I wouldn't be too sure about Ellie missing us,' Beth put in with a teasingly affectionate look at her sister. 'From what I hear, she's going to be far from lonely!'

Ellie felt herself stiffen at her sister's teasing. She had deliberately given Beth the impression that she had definite plans for the rest of her life, knowing that that was the best way to free Beth to live her own life with her husband and baby—but the last thing she had expected was that Beth would publicly announce her intentions in quite this way. And in front of Daniel, of all people!

And, judging by the speculative expression on his face, he was rapidly drawing his own conclusions as to who was to be her future companion—and Peter's familiarity earlier would have added to the impression that he was the man in her life. Oh, well, it was the impression she had hoped to give. There was no future for herself and Daniel anyway...

'Interesting,' Daniel murmured slowly, deliberately holding her gaze with his own for several tension-filled moments before he turned his attention back to the other couple. 'So when is the baby due?' He changed the subject—although that lengthy holding of Ellie's gaze had seemed to say that he was far from finished with the previous one.

There was nothing more to be said. She had no more intention of telling Daniel than she did Beth that her implication about Peter and herself was pure fabrication. It would be better if things were just left as they were and they all got on with their lives. And Daniel's life certainly had nothing to do with her own!

'In six months' time,' James announced, grinning from ear to ear, obviously ecstatic at having his wife back in his arms and at the prospect of the two of them having a child together.

'Congratulations.' Daniel hugged Beth and shook James warmly by the hand. 'Now I suggest we all have lunch together in the hotel restaurant.' He looked at them questioningly.

Ellie inwardly recoiled at the thought of spending any more time with him; it had been bad enough having to see him again this morning, without having to actually eat a meal with him! 'I—'

'I think it would be nice if we all celebrated this happy event,' Daniel continued pointedly.

In other words, if she refused to join them it would look as if she was being difficult, as if she wasn't really happy for the other couple! She could see that Daniel had a point, and knew there was a possibility that her sensitive sister would see it that way if she did refuse, for whatever reason. But, nevertheless, she really didn't want to spend any more time in Daniel's company. And he probably knew that too!

'I was about to say I'll join you in the restaurant in a few minutes,' she said coolly. 'I just have a few things to deal with in the office first.' In truth, she needed a few minutes on her own to prepare herself for spending yet another couple of hours in this man's company!

'Can't they wait?' Beth cajoled, the ecstatic smile on her face telling of her own happiness.

'Five minutes,' Ellie promised, squeezing her sister's hand reassuringly.

'We'll both join you in a few minutes,' Daniel told the other couple authoritatively. 'Order a bottle of champagne,' he instructed James, 'and by the time it arrives we'll be there.'

Ellie looked at him in dismay as Beth and James went off to the dining room together, leaving the two of them alone; this was the last thing she had wanted when she'd made her request for a few minutes' respite. Daniel was the person she needed the respite from!

'Shall we go to the office?' He didn't wait for a reply but firmly clasped her arm and strode purposefully towards the office, taking Ellie with him.

She had decided long ago that this man was far too fond of taking charge of a situation—and usually without regard for other people's feelings. But she had been so taken aback by his suggestion that he was joining her in the office that she hadn't had time to think of a suitable way of putting him off. Which was, she realised, probably exactly what he had hoped for!

God knew what Beth was making of the situation—if her sister had come out of her euphoria long enough to speculate. And if she hadn't done yet she surely would soon. Beth was far from stupid and had barged in on Ellie and Daniel together more than once; her sister would probably, at some stage, after her earlier speculation about Daniel, start to wonder exactly which man Ellie had her plans for the future with—Daniel or Peter! Which was all she needed.

She moved determinedly away from Daniel once they were in the privacy of the office. 'Do you have something private you wish to talk to me about?' She looked across at him with deceptive calm; calm was the last thing she felt around this man!

'Beth and James—'

'Look, Daniel,' she cut in impatiently, 'I've done my best where they are concerned—am still doing so, as far as I'm aware. I want my sister's happiness—'

'That wasn't what I was about to say,' Daniel interrupted smoothly, dark brows raised at the flush of anger on her cheeks.

'Oh?' She was still defensive, not sure she wanted to know what he had been about to say.

'They—Beth especially—seem to think you have plans of your own for the future. I'm interested to know if they include Peter Osborne.'

Ellie gasped; she couldn't help herself. This man had none of the usual social graces, always seemed to go straight for the jugular.

'Well, do they?' he prompted as she didn't make any reply.

She glared at him indignantly. 'I don't think that is any of your business!'

Daniel moved purposefully towards her. 'I'm making it my business.'

'I—'

'Ellie, this nonsense has gone on long enough,' he told her grimly, standing directly in front of her now. 'I've already told you, Osborne isn't the man for you—'

'And I suppose you are?' she cut in challengingly, eyes darkly green.

'I happen to think so, yes.' He more than rose to her challenge, meeting her gaze unflinchingly.

Ellie shook her head. 'Your arrogance is incredible!'

His mouth twisted wryly. 'I'm glad something about me impresses you!'

'Incredible in its magnitude,' she continued impatiently. 'Daniel—'

'I like that,' he said huskily. 'You so rarely use my given name,' he explained at her puzzled look.

That was because there were so many other names for him in her vocabulary! 'I think we should rejoin Beth and James.' She moved determinedly away from him, unnerved by his close proximity, turning to leave.

'Ellie . . .!' Daniel grasped her shoulders from behind, pulling her back against him, his face buried in the thickness of her hair. 'I really need to talk to you. Away from here. Away from any interruptions.'

For a few brief moments she allowed herself the luxury of enjoying his embrace, aware that it was probably the last time she would be this close to him. The truth of the matter was that she dared not be with him 'away from here' and 'away from any interruptions'. She was sure that if she were her resolve where he was concerned would weaken. As it was doing now!

'Daniel, aren't you the one who has constantly told me to stop thinking about myself, to consider other people's happiness?' she reasoned huskily, even though his accusations had been completely unjustified in the first place as far as she was concerned. 'Well, at this moment I have a responsibility to Beth and James.' She turned in his arms, releasing herself to move away a second time. 'We both do,' she added pointedly.

He shook his head. 'Don't we have a responsibility towards ourselves too?'

'At this moment, no.' Her resolve hardened as she thought of Daniel's wedding in two days' time. 'Would you please join Beth and James? I really do have a couple of things to do before I'm free to enjoy lunch.' She met his gaze unflinchingly, determined not to weaken towards him again. She couldn't!

'Ellie—'

'Daniel!' she cut in harshly. 'There will be time for this later, if you really do insist on finishing this conversation.' And, hopefully, later she would be able to tell him to go away and leave her alone.

His expression was grim. 'I really do insist,' he said.

Ellie nodded, having known that he would; Daniel was not a man to give up easily when he had decided on a course of action. She had given herself a couple of hours' respite; hopefully during that time she could come up with the necessary resolve not to get any more involved in his life than she already had been. She certainly had no intention of becoming his mistress once he was married to Angela, and there was no other role he could offer her in his life.

'I'll join you in five minutes,' she promised abruptly. 'The champagne bubbles certainly won't have had time to go flat!' she added in an attempt at lightheartedness; the last thing that was needed was an atmosphere between herself and Daniel at Beth and James's celebration lunch!

Daniel left the office, albeit reluctantly, and Ellie was at last able to breathe again. What was she going to do? How could she possibly get through the next couple of hours in Daniel's company without totally falling apart? More to the point, how could she arrange it so that Daniel no longer wanted to talk to her alone later on?

The minutes speedily ticked by as she tried to think of a way to extricate herself from the torture of being in the company of the man she loved but whom she certainly couldn't have in her life.

And then she had it!

It was all so simple, really. So simple she didn't know why she hadn't thought of it before. The easiest and the most effective way of not having to even eat lunch with Daniel.

Sapphire!

Daniel was so allergic to the perfume that he couldn't bear even to be in the same room as someone who was wearing it. And she had an almost full bottle of it in her bedroom. Added to which, Daniel couldn't help but know she had worn the perfume on purpose—that whatever relationship he was going to propose for them she wasn't interested.

Perfect. Absolutely perfect . . .

*   *   *

She had a chance to observe the three of them un-
noticed as she entered the dining room, and was
pleased to see her sister looking so animated and obviously happy and James appearing nothing like the
unhappy, drunken man she had seen last night. Thank
goodness!

She drank her fill of the sight of Daniel for the last
time, knowing that she loved him—deeply, irrevocably. He was laughing huskily at something James
had said, his blue eyes crinkled at the corners, his
teeth very white and even against his tanned skin. He
looked wonderful, and Ellie knew that this was how
she wanted to remember him. God! After twenty-
seven years she had at last fallen in love, and with
someone so out of reach she couldn't believe she could
have been so stupid.

She straightened her shoulders, forcing a bright
smile to her lips as she crossed the room to join the
happy party. Daniel turned and saw her approach, at
once including her in the warmth of his gaze.

Ellie almost faltered as that searing heat reached
out and engulfed her, feeling herself start to melt. But
she mustn't melt, couldn't become just another
woman in his life, like Joanne and no doubt countless
others. Whatever his reasons he was marrying
someone called Angela—in fact, the conversation
seemed to be about that very person as she reached
the table!

'...sure Angela is going to make a beautiful bride!'
James was saying teasingly.

'I have no doubts on that score,' Daniel answered,
standing up in acknowledgement of Ellie joining them,

resuming his seat as she took hers. 'She looked beautiful at her last three weddings too!'

Ellie gaped at him; the woman he was marrying had been married three times before? And he had been present at all three of the weddings? What—?

'It's after the wedding that the problems seem to beg—' Daniel broke off as his body was racked by a huge sneeze. 'Excuse me,' he dismissed wryly. 'I actually have a theory.' He continued his conversation with the other man. 'And it's that Angela actually enjoys the wedding more than the marriage!'

James gave a throaty laugh, turning to smile at Ellie. 'I'm sorry about this; we really shouldn't be talking in this way about someone you don't even know.' He shook his head in self-rebuke.

'Ellie may not know her,' Daniel mused, 'but she has had an encounter with her on the telephone.' He was still smiling at thoughts of the other woman. 'Even that must have been enough for Ellie to form some sort of an opinion.'

Her opinion was that she wouldn't have liked the other woman no matter whether she was nice or not; how could she possibly like the woman Daniel was to be married to?

James raised his eyes heavenwards. 'Angela is pretty formidable, no matter what the circumstances! You should do something about that cold, Daniel.' He frowned as his friend began to sneeze again.

It was working! The liberal amount of Sapphire she had splashed over herself before joining them was starting to provoke Daniel's allergy.

Daniel looked across at her with eyes that were watering slightly from his fierce bout of sneezing. 'I thought I had,' he said grimly, his meaning not lost on Ellie.

He knew that she was wearing Sapphire, and after their last conversation about the perfume he had to know she had put it on on purpose!

'You certainly don't want a cold for Saturday,' James chided. 'Angela will never forgive you if you go to the wedding with a cold and pass it on to all the guests!'

'I don't have a cold,' Daniel answered him evenly, although that mood was not reflected in the icy look in his eyes. 'I just—' He sneezed again, swearing audibly beneath his breath as he reached into his trouser pocket for a handkerchief. 'Perhaps I should go and take something for this after all,' he murmured grimly once the sneezing had abated for a few seconds. 'I'm sure Ellie has some sort of magic potion put away for just such an occurrence. Don't you?' he directly challenged her.

This wasn't what she had had in mind at all when she had applied the perfume; she had thought that probably the effects of it on him would become so acute that he would excuse himself. Why was it that every encounter she had with Daniel backfired on her?

He stood up abruptly. 'Why don't the two of you order your meal, and we'll rejoin you shortly?' he suggested to the other couple, the meaning of 'we' quickly becoming apparent as he grasped Ellie's arm and pulled her unceremoniously to her feet, his grip actually painful as he let her know his displeasure at what he guessed was a deliberate ploy on her part concerning the perfume. 'Won't we, Ellie?' he prompted harshly before his body was racked by yet another sneeze.

'Yes,' she assured them through gritted teeth, wondering if her arm was actually going to be bruised when Daniel at last released her. But the last thing she wanted to do was cause a scene now that Beth and James had finally got back together. 'I—we shouldn't be long.' She gave a bright, meaningless smile before she was literally dragged from the restaurant.

'Don't speak,' Daniel told her between clenched teeth as they came out into the reception area, his gaze fixed rigidly straight ahead. 'Not a word. Not one damned single word,' he warned harshly as they burst through the door to the private apartment at the back of the hotel. 'The bathroom?' he demanded, not even hesitating in his stride as he moved determinedly across the sitting room.

Ellie turned to him with wide eyes. 'I—'

'Not a word, Ellie,' he said again, in a voice that brooked no argument. 'Just point me in the general direction of the bathroom!'

She did so, recognising a man who had reached his breaking point; God knew what he would do if she proved difficult now! Although why he should want the bathroom she had no idea . . .

She very quickly found out! Still holding tightly onto her arm, Daniel turned on the mixer tap in the shower, his expression still grim as he tested the temperature. If he intended taking a shower, he certainly didn't need her here as his audience—

Wrong assumption. Daniel wasn't the one about to take a shower—Ellie was!

Without even bothering to attempt to remove any of her clothes, Daniel pushed her unceremoniously under the spray of warm water. Ellie's hair was instantly plastered to her head, and her clothes were soon clinging wetly to her body too.

'What the—?'

'I asked you not to wear that perfume near me again,' Daniel reminded her harshly as he pulled her from beneath the water and wrapped a towel about her dripping hair. 'You just didn't listen. But then you never do, do you?' he continued impatiently. 'God, you must be the most cantankerous woman I've ever met in my— Ellie, are you crying?' He suddenly stopped, bending his head slightly so that he could look into her face.

Yes, she was, she realised, as surprised as he as she felt the warm tears falling against her cheeks. Why on earth was she crying? She was crying because she loved this man and he was about to marry someone else!

She looked up at him with huge green eyes, all the fight having deserted her now. 'I put the perfume on because I wanted you to leave,' she admitted chokingly, putting her hands up to her face. 'I wanted you to go away from here. I can't— You—'

'Let it out, Ellie,' Daniel encouraged huskily, all his anger having left him now as he gathered her close in his arms, uncaring that she was wetting him too. 'Just cry. I have a feeling it's a long time since you felt the freedom to do that,' he added regretfully. 'Come on, darling,' he crooned. 'Just let it all out.'

He was right; she couldn't remember the last time she had cried, not matter what the problems had been.

She had had to be so strong for the last couple of years, and it hadn't felt right, in the light of her father's heart condition, to burden her parents with any of the problems that weighed her down so much. And there was never anyone for her to lean on, to unburden herself to. She didn't unburden herself now, but she did cry. She cried and cried, until she felt as if she would never stop. In fact, it was a rather loud hiccup amongst the crying that made her laugh self-consciously at her lack of control.

To her surprise she saw that they weren't in the bathroom any more but had moved through to the sitting room. Ellie was cradled in Daniel's arms as he sat on the sofa and she was on his knee, her face buried against his neck.

'No, don't move,' he instructed huskily as she would have done exactly that. 'I like you exactly where you are,' he added with soft satisfaction.

'But—'

'No buts, Ellie,' he told her firmly, his arms tightening possessively. 'It's time you let someone else take charge for a while. And I'm volunteering—actually I'm pleading for you to let me be the one to do it.' He looked deeply into her eyes.

She was tempted—God, she was so tempted. But— 'What about Angela?' she ventured reluctantly, not really wanting to talk about the other woman at all but knowing that she couldn't just forget she existed.

Daniel frowned. 'What about her?'

Ellie shook her head. 'You have to know—must realise—that she wouldn't like—this.' She indicated their physical closeness.

His expression tightened. 'I am well past the age of caring whether or not my sister approves of anything I do in my life. Especially when it comes to my choice of wife. With her own past record she has no damned right to even voice an opinion—'

'Sister!' It was the only thing that Ellie had really heard in his last statement. Angela was his sister? But if that was the case he couldn't possibly be marrying her in two days' time!

'Yes.' Daniel frowned at her obvious surprise. 'Who did you think she was?'

His fiancée. The woman he loved. The woman he was going to marry.

And then she realised something else he had said a few moments ago—something about his 'choice of wife'...

'Did you mean me?' she gasped in a strained voice.

'Did I mean you what?' Daniel looked puzzled by this whole turn of conversation. 'Ellie, just who did you think Angela was?' he persisted.

The moment of truth. Could she take it, or was she just too much of a coward to take this chance, to risk everything on three little words—'choice of wife'?

She drew in a ragged breath. 'There was talk of a wedding,' she explained in a rush. 'Angela appeared to be the bride. And—'

'And you thought I was the bridegroom?' Daniel finished in a horror-struck voice. 'Believe me, I love Angela because she's my sister, but if she weren't... Angela is bad news for any man stupid enough to get involved with her.' He shook his head disgustedly.

'Ten years ago our father left his business empire jointly to the two of us, and I'm afraid Angela has just never been able to handle it. Too much money at far too young an age, I suppose. The outcome of it is that she chooses wimps for husbands and then wonders why she's bored after a couple of years. I doubt very much that this latest try at the matrimonial stakes will work out any different to the last three!' he added dismissively.

His use of the word 'wimp' reminded Ellie of the time he had taunted her about finding one to marry. She didn't want a wimp; she wanted Daniel!

'But at least Angela's mistakes have taught me to be a damn sight more cautious about my own leap into matrimony.' Daniel settled her more comfortably on his knee, pushing her head down onto his shoulder. 'I've always known I was going to wait for the right woman—and then there would be no going back.'

'Joanne?' she ventured tentatively.

He looked startled, gazing down at her with puzzled eyes. 'Do you have me paired off, woman, with every female you've seen or heard of me being with?' he said impatiently. 'Joanne is my personal assistant.

'It's all a bit damned difficult at the moment, if you must know,' he added grimly. 'The man Angela has chosen to make hubby number four is Joanne's ex-husband! So as you can imagine there is absolutely no love lost between the two women. Which makes it very difficult, because I refuse, despite pressure from my dear sister, to dismiss Joanne as my assistant. She's the best damned worker I've ever had.'

He frowned. 'An example of her efficiency is that she somehow managed to track down Peter Osborne to this hotel,' he confided huskily.

Which meant that James had had nothing to do with it. She was glad about that; it now exonerated her brother-in-law completely in her eyes. 'You know of Peter's past success?' she prompted softly.

Daniel nodded. 'He had one of the most popular restaurants in London, and when Joanne discovered him here, at your hotel, it seemed like too good an opportunity to miss. I thought I could come down here and talk to him and at the same time try to sort out the situation between James and Beth by dealing with the big, bad, ugly sister. Being none of those things, you were not at all what I had been expecting!'

He smiled down at her. 'I managed to thrash quite a lot of that out with James this morning before driving him down here. I know now that a lot of the assumptions I made about you were nowhere near the truth.' He frowned.

'I've never been involved with Peter, you know,' she told him huskily, knowing that they had to get things completely straight between them now. 'He lives in the area to be close to his ex-wife and his daughter. To me he's only ever been a friend.'

Daniel looked relieved by this explanation. 'I'm sure he wishes he could be more.' He shrugged.

'Possibly.' She nodded. 'But Beth has a theory. She believes,' she explained as Daniel looked down at her questioningly, 'that we Thompson women have a once and only love. That once we've fallen that's it.'

Daniel's arms tightened about her. 'James has the same theory about me.' He nodded. 'The thing is, I happen to think he's right. I also know I happen to have found my once and only love with a stubborn red-headed woman named Giselle. Giselle,' he murmured softly. 'It's a very pretty name, my darling. I hope you don't mind if I use it occasionally when we're married. In private, of course. I don't want everyone using my name for you,' he added decisively.

'I—'

'We are getting married, Ellie,' he cut in firmly. 'I've had enough of this time-wasting. I intend to make you my wife as soon as it's legally possible, so get used to the idea,' he announced arrogantly.

'I'm used to it,' she assured him breathlessly, not really knowing whether she ever would be; it seemed too good to be true that Daniel appeared to love her too. Although he hadn't actually said that he did...

'I love you, Daniel,' she told him huskily. 'I love you very much.'

He cradled each side of her face with his hands. 'And you'll marry me?'

'"As soon as it's legally possible".' She chokingly echoed his words.

'I love you, Giselle Thompson. I love you!' he groaned, before his head bent down and his lips finally claimed hers.

There was only the soft sound of their sighs and the murmuring of their voices for a long time after that, and Ellie was so happy, she felt as if she was going to burst with the emotion.

They lay on the sofa, Ellie's face flushed, her lips softly pouting from the kisses they had shared. 'I have a confession to make.' She grimaced up at him. 'That first night you came to the hotel, I was hiding in—'

Daniel put his fingertips over her lips. 'The wardrobe.' He nodded. 'Yes, I know.'

Her gaze was wide on the soft, indulgent look on his face. 'But don't you want to know what I was doing in there?'

He shook his head. 'Not in the least. A wife has to keep some mysteries from her husband. And as long as you aren't wearing Sapphire you can hide in my wardrobe again any time you want to. In fact, I'll probably join you!' he added teasingly.

Ellie returned his kiss with a fervour that had them both spiralling out of control. She loved this man— loved him so much that it seemed to cause an actual physical ache. And then, as Daniel gently possessed her, her physical ache was assuaged, and all the colours of the rainbow exploded inside her head.

Her once and only love...

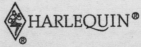

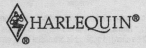